# Computer Ghost

Darling Jade,

No one must know about me but you. I won't be able to talk to you any more if you tell others about me. Don't even tell your mum. She wouldn't understand. No one understands except you. Have you found my package yet? I need it desperately. Don't stop searching until you find it. Time is running out. And remember, not a word to anyone – or you'll never hear from me again. Remember, I'm watching.

Dad.

*Also available in Hippo Mystery:*

**Deadly Dare**
Malorie Blackman

**Cry Danger**
**Disaster Bay**
Ann Evans

HIPPO MYSTERY

# Computer Ghost

Malorie Blackman

*To Neil and Elizabeth, with my love*

Scholastic Children's Books
Commonwealth House, 1–19 New Oxford Street,
London WC1A 1NU, UK
a division of Scholastic Ltd
London ~ New York ~ Toronto ~ Sydney ~ Auckland

First published by Scholastic Ltd, 1997



ISBN 0 590 19657 X


Typeset by TW Typesetting, Midsomer Norton, Somerset
Printed by Cox & Wyman Ltd, Reading, Berks.

10 9 8 7 6 5 4 3 2 1

# Contents

# 1. The Message

To: JDriscoll@JDriscoll.private.uk
From: PDriscoll@PDriscoll.private.uk

Darling Jade,

I miss you so much. You don't know what it's like. I'm so alone here. I can't go forwards, I can't go back. I'm stuck. And I'll be here forever if you don't do something. Please, please help me. I'm desperate. This is the only way I've found of getting through to you. I can't communicate any other way or with anyone else. God knows I've tried. I guess the reason I can talk to you is that you're the only one still listening to me. You're the only one who still believes in me. As far as everyone else is concerned – including your mother – I'm gone for good. Jade, I need your help. Don't let me down.

All my love,

Dad.

## 2. A Brilliant Idea

The noise level in the class was getting louder and louder. Theo stared out of the classroom window beside him, half wondering what had happened to Mrs Daltry. It wasn't like her to be late. Not that he particularly minded that she wasn't here. Mrs Daltry didn't mess about when it came to her class messing about! She was the kind of teacher who took no prisoners! She was very strict, but Theo had to admit that she was also fair. Unlike some of the other teachers, she didn't have favourites and she didn't pick on people without a good reason. Yes, she was definitely one of the better teachers. Not that he'd invite her or any of his teachers to one of his birthday parties!

Theo started in surprise. He was just thinking about her and there she was. He rubbed the grimy glass of the window to get a better look. Mrs Daltry was out in the school grounds talking to the new caretaker, Mr Appleyard. Mr Appleyard had started working at St Christopher's at the beginning of the year and already it was as if he'd been there for ever. Theo wasn't keen on Mr Appleyard. And he wasn't the only one. Mr Appleyard fancied himself as taking over where Hitler had left off. Theo wondered what they were talking about. Hopefully, Mrs Daltry was having a go and giving the caretaker what for! Curious, Theo stood up and opened the window.

"Are you mad?" Ricky rounded on him.

"Theo, shut the window."

"It's freezing!"

"Theo!"

"All right! All right!" Theo shut the window quickly before anyone else could rant in his ear. Oh well! He'd just have to wonder. Still, the longer Mrs Daltry stayed out there, the longer he could stare out at the clear blue

October sky and think. Well, he called it thinking! Mrs Daltry called it wool-gathering. Angela called it daydreaming. Ricky called it space gazing. It was none of those things. It was a time to collect his thoughts, to dream and scheme and use his imagination. It was a time to think about 'what ifs…' and 'suppose that…' And just at that moment the most magnificent 'what if' he'd ever had in his life occurred to him.

Theo turned to Ricky, his eyes wide and shining like car headlights. "Ricky, I've just had a brilliant idea!"

"Even if you do say so yourself!"

"Even if I do say so myself!" Theo agreed with a grin.

"Go on then. What is it?" Ricky urged.

Theo's eyes widened even more in delight at the mere thought of it. The only thing he couldn't figure out was why no one had thought of it sooner.

"Ricky, why don't we start up a detective agency?"

"A what?" Whatever Ricky had been expecting, it hadn't been that!

"A detective agency," Theo repeated. "Right here in the school."

"But … but where would we get our cases from? And besides, the teachers would never allow it."

"Then we won't tell them. This will be a detective agency run by us for the other kids in the school. What d'you think?"

"I don't know. I mean, it *sounds* like a good idea but really we don't know anything about being detectives."

"I do!" Theo contradicted. "I've been reading *How To Be a Detective in 10 Easy Lessons* and *The Detective's Handbook* and *The Spy's Guidebook* and *Young Detective* and *Everything You Ever Wanted to Know About Being a Detective*."

"Wow! Why the sudden interest in sleuthing?" asked Ricky.

"Mum and Dad bought me a detective kit for my birthday." Theo said.

"Oh yeah! You told me." Ricky remembered. "But I thought you weren't terribly impressed by it?"

"I changed my mind," Theo mumbled.

When he caught sight of Ricky's knowing grin, he added testily, "I can change my mind, can't I?"

" 'Course you can," Ricky soothed.

Theo decided not to rise to Ricky's teasing. Especially since Theo knew it was his own fault. He remembered how he'd whined and complained about the present his parents had bought him. But once he'd sat down and started reading all the accompanying blurb and taken a good look at what was actually in the kit, it'd turned out to be not so bad after all. It fact it had turned out to be very interesting – not that Theo would ever admit that to his mum and dad. Not after the way he'd moaned at them for buying him something so feeble!

"So what d'you think of my idea?" Theo persisted.

"Hadn't I better read all that detective stuff too before we start offering our services as detectives?" said Ricky.

"Yeah, yeah!" Theo waved Ricky's observation aside with an impatient hand. "But what about the cases we're going to solve? We'll only pick really interesting, exciting cases. Only cases that are going to be a real challenge. We'll be like Sherlock Holmes and Watson, Poirot and Hastings, Batman and Robin. We'll be..."

"OK class, settle down. The cat's back now!" Mrs Daltry swept into the room, followed by a man Theo had never seen before. The man was tall, with mid-brown hair swept back off his head and a slightly lighter, short-cut, neat beard. His piercing ice-blue eyes looked as if they wouldn't miss much.

"I said settle down. Or we can all practise being quiet during the lunch break later," Mrs Daltry said, annoyed.

Instant silence.

"That's better. Now this is Mr Dove. He's going to be taking over this class from next week for the rest of the term."

Murmurs immediately erupted throughout the classroom. Angela put up her hand.

"Yes, Angela." Mrs Daltry sighed as if she knew what was coming.

"Where are you going to be, Mrs Daltry?" Angela asked.

Theo smiled. That was Angela. As blunt as

ever. Always asking the questions that no one else dared.

"I am going away and I won't be back until the New Year," Mrs Daltry said.

"Where are you going?"

"If you must know, I'm going to Canada for six weeks."

"How come?"

"I won a prize and this is the only time the prize organizers will let me go. I have to go next week or I can't go at all."

"How did you win...?"

"I think that's quite enough, Angela. If you went to university and did a degree in nosiness, you'd get a first!" Mrs Daltry interrupted firmly. "Now then everyone, Mr Dove will be sitting in with us for the rest of the week, just to see how we do things."

"I'm looking forward to it." Mr Dove directed his smile around the class.

"He doesn't need a week for that. It'll only take about five minutes," Ricky whispered to Theo.

"Thank you, Ricky but when I want your opinion I'll ask for it," said Mrs Daltry.

Ricky and Theo stared at her. How on earth had she heard that? They were sitting towards the back of the class.

"She's got ears like a bat!" Theo whispered, his voice so low that even he could barely hear it.

"And don't you forget it, Theo!" Mrs Daltry smiled.

Theo decided to give up. Much as he was dying to discuss his new idea with Ricky, he certainly didn't want to risk having to sit outside the staff room at lunch time. He'd just have to put his idea on hold until after the lesson.

But it *is* a brilliant idea, he thought to himself. And he felt sure that everyone in the class – no, everyone in the entire *school* would immediately agree with him.

"A detective agency. Are you nuts?" Colin roared with laughter.

Theo tried not to let his annoyance show but he failed. All day, he'd been getting exactly the same reaction. Was he really the only one in the school with any *vision?*!

"Oh, come on, Theo." Colin wiped the tears from his eyes. "You must admit that it's a bit of a bizarre idea."

"No, I don't admit any such thing," Theo replied testily. "What's wrong with it?"

"Well, for a start, what d'you know about being a detective?" asked Jack. "And secondly, this isn't New York. This is St Christopher's! What crimes do you expect to solve in our school?"

"The only crimes here are the school dinners," Colin added.

"You'd be surprised. There are lots of mysteries that go on in this school," said Theo.

"Like what?" asked Ricky.

Theo scowled at his friend. Whose side was he on? Ricky got the unsubtle hint and looked suitably contrite.

"Just give us a chance – OK?" Ricky said quickly. "You'll be amazed."

"I'm amazed already," Jack said. "Theo, you've come up with some weird ideas in your time but this is the best yet."

Colin immediately started laughing again. And off Jack and Colin went to their first lesson of the afternoon. Ricky and Theo trailed behind them. Theo couldn't believe it, he really couldn't. He had thought they'd be inundated with cases. He really believed they'd have to pick and choose. After he'd had the idea in Mrs Daltry's class that morning, he spent the rest of the lesson going over in his mind the detective techniques he'd learnt and working out the best way to keep track of the many cases they were bound to get. He'd even mentally practised turning down those clients unlucky enough to have boring cases.

"I'm so sorry, but we're just too busy… Our caseload is phenomenal, astronomical, extra-ordinary, sensational … BIG!!"

"We don't seem to be getting very far," said Ricky.

"Don't worry. I'm not giving up," Theo said with determination.

But even as he spoke, he realized that starting his detective agency was going to be more of an uphill struggle than he'd ever imagined.

"We'll just have to convince everyone that they really need us," said Theo, thoughtfully.

The question was, how?

## 3. Reality Like Rot

"I can't believe this place, I really can't," Theo bristled.

"You'll just have to give everyone a chance to get used to the idea," said Ricky.

"I think it's a good idea," Angela added.

Theo, Ricky and Angela were all walking home together. The day had turned out to be a raging disappointment for Theo. He'd stood outside the school gates, trying to convince everyone who came out that his detective agency was going to be the best thing since salt and vinegar crisps. He still couldn't believe the apathy his brilliant idea had been met with. Those who hadn't laughed in his face didn't seem to care much about the idea one way or the other. Reality, like rot, was beginning to set in.

"I can't understand it. I thought people would be queuing up to use us." Theo couldn't keep the frustration out of his voice. "Maybe we should advertise?"

"How?"

"I could print off some ads using Mum and Dad's computer tonight," said Theo. "Something along the lines of – 'Got a problem? Come and see the only ones who can really help you out. Theo and Ricky.' Something like that."

"You'll have to do better than that if you want people to take you seriously. You'll need a better name for your detective agency than 'Theo and Ricky's'! That sounds like a restaurant!" said Angela. "And your ad will have to be eye-catching but discreet. Obvious yet tasteful. Bold yet sincere."

Ricky and Theo exchanged a look.

"I'm serious," said Angela. "Anyway, I doubt if you'll get many girls asking for your help."

That stopped Theo dead in his tracks.

"Why not?"

"'Cause you're two boys. You can't be

expected to deal with *girl* problems."

"Why not?" Theo's frown deepened.

"'Cause you're a boy. You won't understand the way we girls do things. The way we think and feel. Girl problems need to be handled in a very special way."

"What a load of rubbish!" Ricky scoffed. "We both helped you with your problem not too long ago."

"Too right," Theo agreed.

"Yes, but that was a one-off. I'm telling you, you won't get any girl clients – not unless you have a girl helping you out with your cases," said Angela.

"Ah!" Theo said, as the penny dropped. "We do have a girl helping us. You!"

"I thought you'd never ask," Angela grinned.

"Why didn't you just come right out and say that you wanted to be part of our detective agency?" asked Ricky.

"I just did!" Angela smiled.

"I hate it when people don't come out and say what they mean," Ricky complained, more to himself than to anyone else. He added, "So what should we do now?"

"You two need to read all the blurb I have on how to be a detective," Theo said decisively. He dug into his duffel bag and dug out some of his detective manuals which he always carried with him now. "*Don't* lose these," he ordered, as he handed them over. "Meanwhile, I'll make up some flyers advertising our services and print them off on Mum and Dad's computer."

"They don't mind you becoming a detective?" asked Ricky.

"I haven't actually passed the idea by them yet," Theo admitted. "But I'm sure they'll say yes."

"And if they don't?" Angela raised an eyebrow.

Theo had a think about it. "They won't say no," he decided.

"How can you be so sure?" Angela persisted.

"I just know. That's all."

Angela and Ricky exchanged a smile.

"You're not going to tell them, are you?" Angela grinned.

"Nope!" Theo replied. "And no one likes a know-it-all!"

* * *

Theo leaned forward and viewed the computer screen critically. It didn't look *too* bad. His advertisement was all the things Angela had recommended – eye-catching yet discreet, obvious yet tasteful, bold yet sincere.

"Theo, you're a genius!" he murmured.

But just to make sure, he'd print off one to see how it looked on paper. Theo used his mouse to click on the <Print> option and waited impatiently for the printer to finish.

**WE CAN HELP!**

- **Lost your homework?**
- **Can't find your school bag?**
- **Want to know if that certain someone fancies you?**

**We offer a discreet, confidential service. Get in touch with Theo, Ricky or Angela**

| Missing Items | Fraud / Con Tricks | Help With Your Love Life (Within Reason!) | Missing Animals | Theft! | Missing People | Any Problem Tackled | Strictly Confidential | No Job Too Large or Too Small | Weeks Of Experience! |
|---|---|---|---|---|---|---|---|---|---|

Theo nodded as he studied the flyer carefully. He sat back, satisfied.

"Theo, you're a definite genius," he told himself again.

If this didn't get them some clients with cases to solve, then nothing would!

## 4. Ignoring You

To: PDriscoll@PDriscoll.private.uk
From: JDriscoll@JDriscoll.private.uk

Dear Dad,

I want to help you, I really do. But I don't know how. You'll have to tell me what you want me to do. Please don't think that I've been ignoring you – I haven't. It's just that it's very difficult to use the PC at the moment. I have to wait until Mum's asleep, or out. She's terrified the same thing will happen to me that happened to you. I've tried to tell her that it won't, but she won't listen.

You don't know how it feels to run to the computer each morning hoping you'll have sent me a message. It's the only thing I have to look forward to. (I have to wait until Mum's having her bath, but if you've sent me a message, it's always worth the wait). Write soon, Dad. All my love, Jade.

## 5. The Surprise

"Everyone's talking about your flyers," Ricky whispered to Theo.

Theo beamed back at him. "I knew they'd get a response."

"Let's just hope that none of the teachers get hold of one," Ricky said, worried.

"Don't worry. I told everyone they weren't to let any of the teachers see them."

"That doesn't mean they won't," Ricky pointed out.

They had no time to discuss it further as Mrs Daltry walked into the classroom with Mr Dove. Mr Dove smiled all around again before sitting on a chair against the wall. Theo frowned as he watched their new teacher. The man was a definite wafer! No taste nor flavour! He looked like he wouldn't say boo to a worm, never mind a goose!

I bet he's even more boring than Mrs Daltry, Theo thought sourly.

"Mr Dove will be taking you for your double lesson this afternoon as he's raring to go." Mrs Daltry looked at Mr Dove like he had only one marble left in his head. "So I don't want any nonsense now or this afternoon."

And with that, Mrs Daltry didn't waste any time but got straight down to it.

"Does anyone know what 'paranormal' means?"

A few hands flew upwards. A couple more struggled up. The rest stayed down.

"Ricky?" Mrs Daltry prompted.

"It means things that are not quite normal. Things that are above and beyond and outside normal," Ricky replied.

"Such as?"

"Like being able to move things with your mind ... er ... telekinesis, and leaving your body while you're still alive - that's astral projection – and mind-reading and vampires and people who can stretch their bodies through narrow ventilation shafts and..."

"Thank you, Ricky. I think we all get the idea," Mrs Daltry said quickly. She added with a smile, "You seem to know a lot about it."

"I like to watch *The X-Files*, miss!" Ricky grinned.

The rest of the class tittered.

"Hhmm!" Mrs Daltry sniffed. "Now I know why you never hand in your homework on a Monday morning. Too busy watching the telly late on a Sunday evening."

Ricky bent his head, ruefully acknowledging that he was guilty as charged.

"The dictionary definition of paranormal phenomena is that which is outside the scope of the known laws of nature or normal objective investigation," Mrs Daltry continued. "That's just a long winded way of saying anything which can't be explained using our known laws of science and nature."

Theo listened to the teacher, surprised. For once, what she was saying was actually *interesting*! What had come over her? An interesting lesson with Mrs Daltry was a paranormal event in itself!

"Does anyone here believe in ghosts?" asked Mrs Daltry.

Immediately, Ricky's arm shot up. Theo stared at him, stunned. Ricky looked at Theo, had a quick look around, then his arm came down faster than a felled tree. Two surprises in less than two minutes. It must have something to do with the subject they were discussing!

"You really believe in ghosts?" Theo still couldn't believe it.

"Yeah! So?" Ricky scowled.

Theo had another look around. Very few people had their hands up and those that did were rapidly reconsidering it.

"Why d'you believe in ghosts then?" Theo asked.

"Theo, who's giving this lesson? Me or you?" Mrs Daltry asked.

"Sorry," Theo mumbled.

"So Ricky, why d'you believe in ghosts?" Mrs Daltry gave Theo a wry smile before turning to Ricky.

"I just do, that's all," Ricky replied.

Theo recognized that tone. Ricky was sorry he'd ever admitted to it.

"Have you ever seen a ghost?" Mrs Daltry asked.

Ricky licked his lips carefully. "Er ... no," he answered in a tiny voice.

Mrs Daltry moved on to one of the others who had put their hand up.

Theo elbowed Ricky in the ribs.

"Ricky, *have* you seen a ghost?" he whispered.

"Shush! I'll tell you after the lesson," Ricky replied softly.

"I'd appreciate that." Mrs Daltry appeared from nowhere to whisper in Ricky's ear.

She carried on with the lesson, talking about imagination and science and how science fiction often turned into science fact. Mrs Daltry then went on to discuss the power of the imagination in the sciences as well as in the arts. Theo listened with half an ear. As interesting as it was, it still couldn't compare to the fact that his friend Ricky believed in *ghosts*. If Theo hadn't heard it with his own ears, he'd never have believed it. He studied Ricky avidly.

"Stop that!" Ricky hissed.

"Stop what?"

"Stop glaring at me as if I've just sprouted another head or something."

"This *is* a lesson about the paranormal," Theo teased.

"I mean it!" Ricky said, annoyed.

"I'm not staring."

"Yes, you are."

"I ... er, well, maybe just a little. You surprised me, that's all," Theo admitted. "I would've said you're the last person in the world to believe in all that stuff."

"Theo, let me know when you've finished so that I can begin again," Mrs Daltry said testily.

"Sorry. I've finished now," Theo said quickly.

"I'm glad to hear it." Mrs Daltry's tone was saccharine. "And maybe you'd like to sit outside the staff room for the whole of this afternoon's break. That way you'll have plenty of time to come up with a reason why you felt it necessary to chat whilst I was trying to teach."

"But Mrs Daltry..."

Mrs Daltry raised a hand to halt Theo's objections. "OK then. But the next time I catch you talking that's exactly what will happen."

Theo pursed his lips, determined not to say another word. Mrs Daltry might be one of the better teachers in the school but sometimes she could be a real bovine entity! A real bovine entity and three quarters!

# 6. The Question

"Ricky, when did you see a ghost then?" The question was out of Theo's mouth the moment they set foot out of the classroom.

The lunchtime buzzer had sounded but Theo's class were all on second lunch so they had half an hour to wait before they could eat.

"What makes you think I've seen one?" Ricky asked.

"Oh, come on!" Theo was insulted. "*How* long have we been friends? I know there's something you're not telling me."

"Well..." Ricky began reluctantly.

"Wait for me then." Angela came running up. "Have you two done your French homework?"

"Yep!"

"Yeah. Why?"

"Can I borrow it?" Angela asked hopefully. "I didn't manage to finish mine."

"Never mind that now," Theo dismissed. "Ricky was just about to tell us about a ghost he saw."

"You really saw a ghost?" Angela stared.

"It was ages ago when Mum took me up to Scotland after her divorce," Ricky began. "We were staying in this bed and breakfast place that used to be a mansion. One morning I was in the dining-room and..."

"Ricky, did you mean it?"

Ricky turned at the tap on his shoulder. Jade stood immediately behind him, her expression deadly serious. Theo frowned at her. She'd interrupted them just as Ricky was getting to what promised to be the good bit! Mr Dove walked past and gave them all a friendly smile. Everyone shut up until the teacher had turned the corner.

"Did I mean what?" Ricky asked.

"Do you really believe in ghosts?" Jade asked.

"Yes," Ricky said. "And if you're going to laugh, you can go away and do it somewhere else."

"I'm not going to laugh," Jade replied quietly.

Theo studied Jade's face – there was no sign that she was on a wind-up.

"Theo, do you believe in ghosts too?" Jade asked.

Theo frowned. "I don't know. I haven't made up my mind about it one way or the other."

Jade turned to Angela. "What about you?"

"No," Angela's answer was immediate. "No, I don't."

"You don't think ... something else, some other part of us lives on when our bodies die?" Jade asked.

"I don't think so. I think when you're dead, you're dead and that's it – end of story." Angela shrugged.

"And you, Theo?"

"I'd have to think about it."

"Think about it now," Jade urged.

Angela, Theo and Ricky exchanged a

questioning look. What was all this about? Why was Jade suddenly so interested in talking to them about Mrs Daltry's lesson?

"Come on, Theo. What d'you think?" Jade prompted.

Theo blinked with surprise. "Er ... I don't know. I think ... maybe some part of us might live on after our bodies die, but I certainly don't believe in ghosts in white sheets that go, 'Ooo-ooooh!'"

A trace of a smile flickered across Jade's face.

"I don't believe in ghosts in white sheets either," she said.

"But you do believe in other kinds of ghosts?" Theo prompted.

"D'you think ghosts can use things in this world to communicate with us?" Jade answered Theo's question with one of her own.

"What sort of things?"

"I don't know." Jade shrugged nonchalantly. "Telephones, televisions, computers, that sort of thing."

"I've no idea. But I wouldn't have thought so," Theo replied. "What's this all about?"

"I was just wondering." Jade shrugged, but Theo wasn't fooled by her fake nonchalance for a second.

He watched the uncertainty race across Jade's face. Jade was a quiet girl who kept herself to herself as far as Theo could tell. She was certainly one of the prettiest in the class. She had huge, brown eyes, a ready smile and plaited black hair which was always an immaculate work of art. But over the last two weeks she'd walked around as if she was Atlas, with the weight of the world on her shoulders. Whatever it was that was troubling her, Theo certainly hadn't expected her to talk about ghosts.

"Well? We're listening," Angela prompted, after a glance at the others.

"It's just that ... no, never mind!" Jade broke off quickly.

"Go on."

There was a long silence before Jade spoke.

"My dad ... talks to me..." Jade's voice grew quieter and quieter before tailing off altogether.

Theo gasped. After a quick glance at his friends' puzzled faces, Theo realized that they didn't realize what Jade had just said.

"So? Why *wouldn't* your dad talk to you?" Angela said, confused.

"It doesn't matter." Jade shook her head and started off down the corridor. "Forget I said anything."

"But Jade..."

They all watched Jade's rapidly retreating back.

"Did I miss something? Why on earth wouldn't her dad talk to her?" Angela asked.

"Angela," Theo said, "Jade's dad died two months ago."

# 7. Bullet

Angela stared at Theo, thinking she'd misheard. From the look on his face, she knew she hadn't. "But that doesn't make any sense. He can't have died."

"He did. He was found slumped over his PC in their house. They reckon he had a heart attack – if I remember rightly," Theo explained.

"How come you know so much about it and I don't?" Angela asked.

"My mum works for the same company that Jade's dad used to work for," Theo explained.

"How come you never told me about Jade's dad?" Angela asked, annoyed.

"Can you keep a secret?"

"Yes," Angela replied, leaning forwards eagerly.

"So can I," said Theo. "It was up to Jade to tell you, not me."

Angela frowned, but Theo knew she'd got the message.

Ricky was still looking down the corridor after Jade. Theo hadn't often seen that serious look on his friend's face, but when he did he knew that Ricky had made up his mind to do something and there was nothing that would stop him.

"D'you think Jade's dad is trying to communicate with her in some way?" Ricky asked.

"Is that what Jade was talking about?" said Angela.

"I don't know, but I think we need to talk to her," Ricky decided. "We need to find out exactly what's going on."

"This afternoon I'd like to talk about how all our lives have been changed due to computers. We're lucky enough to be in the middle of a technological revolution and just as machines changed everyone's lives during the Industrial Revolution, so things for us will never be the same again." Mr Dove walked up and down, up and down between the class tables. "Can anyone tell me where you might find computer and microchip technology in your home?"

Hands shot up, including Ricky's. Theo glanced down at his watch. There was ages to go yet before the end of the lesson. Mr Dove was a typical teacher. He was taking a riveting subject like computing and making it as dry as a cream cracker! Eventually Mr Dove waved everyone quiet amid the cries of "Microwaves?" and "The video recorder, sir?"

"Hands up all those whose parents' jobs are in some way related to computers?" asked the teacher.

More and more hands began to rise into the air. Theo looked around with interest. His mum worked in the marketing department of a computer company. Did that count? Theo decided that it did and put his hand up. Looking around, he saw that Jade had also put up her hand. Did her mum work with computers as well then?

"Jade, how is your mum or dad involved in computing?" asked Mr Dove.

"My dad's a software engineer. He designs games," Jade replied.

Ricky and Theo exchanged a glance.

"Oh? Any games I might have heard of?" Mr Dove smiled.

"*Planet of the Anvil.*"

Mr Dove frowned. "I don't think I've heard of that one."

"That was Dad's new one." Jade lowered her gaze.

"When will that be available?" asked the teacher.

"D-Dad never finished it," Jade replied miserably.

Theo held his breath as he waited for Mr Dove to ask why. But to his surprise the teacher didn't ask. All he said was, "That's a shame." Then he went on to ask the same question of Amber.

"This is too weird," Ricky whispered to Theo. "Jade talks about her dad as if he's still

... alive."

"I was just thinking that," Theo whispered back. "She mixes up the past and the present tense – did you notice?"

Ricky nodded. "I'm just surprised that Mr Dove didn't."

"Would you like to share your comments with the rest of the class? It's Ricky, isn't it?"

"I was just saying that even some washing machines and tumble dryers have microchips in them now. My mum just bought a washing machine and you can delay the time it starts at by up to nine hours. I was just wondering if that built-in clock mechanism is an example of an actual microchip?" Ricky said without hesitation.

Mr Dove smiled. "That's a very good question, Ricky. And it leads us on to a very interesting point..."

Theo elbowed Ricky under the table. Very nicely done! Ricky nudged back acknowledging the 'Well done!' contained within Theo's bony elbow. Theo turned to look at Jade again. It seemed to him that she was stuck in the middle of a kind of no man's land. Her dad had died, and yet he wasn't quite dead because, according to Jade, he was still talking to her. What did Jade's dad say? What did he *want*? Or was this someone's sick idea of a joke? No wonder Jade was so unhappy. No wonder she mixed up the past and the present. For her they were almost the same thing. Theo turned back to the front of the class and mentally shook his head. He wouldn't like to be in Jade's shoes. Not for all the CD games in the local shopping precinct.

"Angela! Why are we going in there?" Ricky asked impatiently.

"I need to print out my homework," Angela snapped. "It'll take two minutes. Anyway, why're you in such a hurry?"

"I want to catch up with Jade before she goes home," Ricky replied. He glanced down at his watch. "She's talking to Mrs Driscoll at the moment."

"I won't be long," Angela insisted.

"I'll wait for you out here," said Ricky. "I don't want to miss her."

"Suit yourself." Angela shrugged.

Theo and Angela walked into the computer room. Theo frowned at Angela. School was over for another day and truth to tell, Theo wanted to go home. It was chicken and rice for dinner tonight, one of his favourites. He looked around. Three times a week, after school, Mrs Sumonu ran the computer club. And even though it was an after school activity, the room was still three-quarters full. Theo wasn't surprised by the people he saw either. He could've guessed who'd be part of the computer club and he would have got ninety-nine per cent of them right. And the first person he would've guessed at was Toby, better known as Bullet. Theo eyed Bullet warily. Bullet's nickname was well-deserved. You only had to be around him for a minute or so before wanting to leave with the haste of a speeding bullet – and Theo should know. Toby sat directly behind him in class.

The trouble was – Toby was boring and three-quarters!

He ate, slept, lived and breathed computers. Theo loved computers himself, but even he knew where to draw the line. It wasn't even as if Bullet was into computer games. No, he was into the serious stuff like writing his own programs – to do nothing that would be of any interest to anyone except Bullet as far as Theo could see. Bullet was also into the hardware side of computers. He was riveted by how computers and modems and screens looked and worked from the inside out. Theo couldn't understand it. As long as the computer worked on the outside, who cared what it looked like on the inside!

"Angela, come on, then," Theo urged. "I thought you wanted to print off something."

Angela looked around, her head moving this way and that.

"There you are, Angela." Theo pointed to the nearest unoccupied seat in front of a PC.

"No..." Angela continued to look around. "There's a seat over there."

"But that chair is next to Bullet," Theo whispered conspiratorially. "You don't want to sit next to him, d'you?"

A deep, burning blush crept across Angela's face. "I don't care about that. I just want to use a PC."

"So what's wrong with that one?" Theo pointed to the PC he'd indicated earlier.

"Because I like that one over there," Angela replied, agitated.

Confused, Theo looked from Angela to Bullet and back again. A slow, knowing smile crept across his face.

"You..."

"No, I don't – before you say it," Angela denied vehemently.

"You *do*!" Theo was astounded. "You fancy Bullet! You need to get your eyes tested asap, and whilst you're at it, you'd better let them look for your brain as well. I think it's fallen out of your ears."

"I don't fancy Bullet," Angela hissed. "And don't you dare tell anyone that I do."

"Your secret is safe with me," Theo beamed.

"Oh, shut up," Angela snapped. And with that she marched off.

Theo couldn't resist it. He sauntered across to sit on the other side of Bullet. What on earth did Angela see in him? Bullet was long and gangly and had more pimples than a zit cream ad on the telly. He didn't think much of Angela's taste.

"Hi, Bullet. How're you?" Angela asked, still looking at her own computer screen.

"Huh? Er... yes... er, I'm OK," Bullet spluttered.

Angela swivelled in her chair to face him. For the first time she saw Theo was sitting on the other side of Bullet and the instant scowl on her face could've curdled milk. Bullet obviously thought the look was directed at him. He sat back in his chair, terrified.

"Bullet, don't you just hate it when certain people butt in and won't mind their own business?" Angela hissed.

"Er ... pardon? No ... yes ... I guess."

Giving Theo the filthiest look she could muster, Angela focused all her attention on Bullet.

"So what're you working on, Bullet, I mean, Toby?"

Bullet looked surprised, not to mention flattered.

"I ... er, well actually, I'm working on a master program to solve things." Bullet's voice grew quieter but more steady as he started to talk about his favourite subject.

A program to solve things! Theo snorted with disgust. He might've guessed Bullet was writing a program to do his homework.

"What sort of things are you trying to solve?" Angela prompted. "D'you mean things like science and maths questions, like equations and angles and areas and stuff like that?"

Theo could've sworn that Angela actually batted her eyelashes at Bullet. Pass the sick bag!

Bullet's eyes gleamed. "Not exactly," he lowered his voice so that Theo had to strain to hear him. "I'm writing a program to solve crimes."

Angela stared at him. And she wasn't the only one.

"You're joking," she said, uncertainly.

Bullet shook his head emphatically. "No, I'm not – I promise. I reckon that if you input enough data and that data is analysed and interpreted in the right way, then there's no reason why a computer shouldn't solve crime problems just as easily as it solves maths problems."

Theo couldn't help it. He was actually interested in what Bullet was saying! First Mrs Daltry, and now Bullet. This was turning out to be an X-files kind of day and no mistake. Surreptitiously, he tried to draw his chair closer to Bullet's.

"So how does this program work? How do you input all the necessary information and how do you know when you've put in enough and..."

"Hang on! Hang on!" Bullet raised a protesting hand. "I'm just finishing off the program now. Then I'll need a real, live crime to input to test it properly."

"Can I see how it would work?" Angela pulled her chair closer to Bullet. So did Theo. Bullet turned, startled, as Theo's head suddenly appeared over his shoulder.

"Don't mind me," Theo smiled. "I'd just like to see how this works too."

"I ... er ... well, I don't ... er..."

"Angela! Theo! We have to get going." Ricky popped his head around the door.

"Just a minute." Theo waved Ricky off impatiently.

"No. We have to go now or we'll miss her." Ricky insisted.

Reluctantly Theo stood up, followed by Angela.

"I'll have to catch up with you later." Angela smiled at Bullet.

Pass two sick bags! Theo thought with disgust. As they made their way out of the computer room, Theo turned to Angela.

"Why didn't you just fall down at his feet and kiss them?" he sniffed. "You made a real fool of yourself there."

"Theo, I've told you before and I'll tell you again." Angela rounded on him. "Mind your own business."

## 8. The Offer

"Why're you lot hanging around out here?"

Angela, Theo and Ricky looked at each other. Each of them had the same expression on their faces. Mini Hitler had arrived and from the belligerent look on his face they could tell he was in the mood to throw his weight around.

"We're waiting for someone, Mr Appleyard," Ricky explained.

"Who?"

"A friend."

"Hhmm!" Mr Appleyard looked at them out of the corner of narrowed eyes. "Well, why can't you wait for them somewhere else?"

Theo glared at him. What *was* his problem? They were outside the school gates and they weren't causing any trouble, for goodness' sake.

"We won't be much longer. Our friend is just coming," Ricky soothed the caretaker.

"Hhmm! All right then," said Mr Appleyard. And he turned to walk back to the school building, just as a few others left the premises.

"That man needs to get a life!" Theo sniffed.

"Too right!" Angela agreed emphatically.

"Hi Jade. Are you OK?"

Startled, Jade turned around. She was even more startled when she saw who had asked the question. Ricky. And just behind him stood Angela and Theo.

"Where did you suddenly appear from?" Jade asked.

"We've been waiting for you," said Ricky.

Ricky, Theo and Angela had been standing outside the school gates for at least ten minutes. It was drizzling and from the look of it, the weather was going to get a lot worse. Grey clouds filled the sky. The kind of clouds that were dark, almost charcoal grey, but which seemed to be lit by candlelight from within. Theo hoped it would pour with rain. He liked the rain.

"I didn't see you," said Jade.

"I'm not surprised. You were in a world of your own," Ricky smiled.

"What's the matter?" Jade asked with narrowed eyes. "What d'you want?"

"I ... er, I wanted to say I was sorry to hear about your dad," Ricky said.

Jade turned to Theo, then back to Ricky. Theo shifted from foot to foot with unease. "My dad died a couple of months ago. What suddenly brought this on?" she asked.

"I just wanted to say that ... if you ever need any help with anything, then – I'm here. We all are."

"Are you serious?" Jade raised her eyebrows.

"Totally," Ricky replied.

"This is just so you can get a client for one of your detective cases, isn't it?"

"It has nothing to do with that," Ricky denied.

"If I needed any help – which I don't – what makes you think I'd ask you of all people?" said Jade.

Theo was furious for his friend and even Angela, who was better at hiding her true feelings than Theo, gasped at Jade's nerve. But to Theo's surprise Ricky merely smiled.

"Maybe because I'm so unlikely," said Ricky. "Then, no matter what you tell me, you know I won't reply in the same way as everyone else."

Jade frowned but didn't reply.

"Jade, I recognize that look on your face. It reminds me of how I must've looked – and felt – when … when I was in trouble a while ago. So I just wanted to say, if you need someone to talk to, I'm here. We all are." Ricky turned round to Theo and Angela. "Come on, gang. Let's leave Jade to think it over."

They all trooped past Jade in silence, leaving her to watch them. Ricky turned round after a few steps.

"Oh, and another thing. I believe in ghosts," he said easily.

And with that he carried on walking. Theo

couldn't help it. He turned and gave Jade a reproachful look before falling into step with Ricky. She didn't have to be quite so nasty.

"Jade's really rude and sarky. She reminds me a bit of you," Theo told Angela.

"Thanks a lot!" Angela was definitely *not* impressed.

"No, I mean how you used to be," Theo amended hastily.

"Thanks a lot!"

"No, I mean…"

"Theo, give up while you're behind!" Ricky laughed.

Theo side-stepped a couple of paces away from Angela, giving her a wary look. That hadn't come out right at all. "Ricky, you still haven't told us about the ghost you saw when you were on holiday," Theo reminded him, anxiously changing the subject.

"Oh yes. Where was I? I remember. Well, it was late morning and..."

"Ricky, wait."

Theo sighed as Jade came running up to them. It didn't look like he'd ever hear the end of Ricky's story.

"I ... er ... I would like to talk to you." Jade looked down at the front of her left shoe which moved nervously back and forth over the glistening pavement as if she was trying to work a hole in the concrete. "I don't know how to say this..."

"Is it about your dad?" Ricky prompted.

Jade nodded quickly, her expression grateful. Someone else had brought up the subject of her dad first.

"He ... he talks to me."

Theo's eyes narrowed. He couldn't help it. If this wasn't a wind-up, then he had no idea what Jade was up to. Was she serious? She couldn't be... There were no such things as ghosts. Not that kind of ghost. Not really. Maybe soldiers who died in wars and all those people in the French Revolution who had been guillotined, maybe their ghosts still floated about somewhere, but not everyday people. That was just silly. The more Theo thought about it, the more unlikely he thought the whole thing.

"Theo, I know what that look on your face means." Jade shook her head. "I don't blame you. I didn't believe it myself at first."

"What does your dad say to you?" Angela asked.

"He doesn't actually *say* anything."

"But you just said he talks to you."

"Yes, but I meant he..." Jade sighed. "Look, this would be easier if I could show you what I mean. I only live a few minutes away. If you three aren't in a rush to get home, I could show you what I'm talking about. It'll only take five minutes."

Theo sighed inwardly. He could almost smell his dad's rice and chicken, but he was no closer to getting to it. His stomach rumbled in protest, but Theo ignored it. He looked at Ricky and Angela and shrugged.

"Yeah. OK." Ricky spoke for all of them.

A relieved smile spread slowly over Jade's face. Theo was startled to realize that he hadn't seen Jade smile in a very, very long time. They walked to Jade's house in silence. A strange, embarrassed hush descended over all of them. It was as if each of them had only just realized exactly *why* they were going to Jade's home. Jade's dad – a *ghost* – actually spoke to her and

Jade was going to show them. Theo turned to Jade with a sudden frown, suspicion in his eyes. If Jade was winding them up, then he'd never speak to her again. Never, ever. How would he ever live it down if the word got out that he went to Jade's house to meet her dead father? Jade turned her head to look at him and Theo quickly looked away.

"I'm not lying, Theo," Jade said quietly.

"I never said you were," Theo answered defensively.

"No?"

Theo looked away, feeling guilty and annoyed because of it. Not for the first time, he wished that what he was thinking wasn't always so obviously apparent on his face. It had got him into trouble more than once before. He just couldn't help feeling like they were all inside a joke, just waiting for the punch line. He didn't want the punch line to be at his expense, that was all.

Walking along, Theo began to feel distinctly uncomfortable. He couldn't put his finger on it and yet the hairs on his nape were slowly standing to attention. Frowning deeply, Theo turned around. The road behind them was clear. There were just a couple of cars on the road and yet Theo couldn't shake the wary feeling creeping over him. It was as if … as if they were being watched… Theo turned his head again quickly.

"Theo, what's the matter?" asked Ricky.

"Nothing. Nothing," Theo denied quickly.

He was imagining things, letting his imagination gallop away with him. And no wonder with all this talk about ghosts and ghouls and things that went bump in the night. And yet…

*Were they being followed?*

"Theo…?" Ricky prompted.

"It's OK. I'm all right. Nothing's the matter," Theo replied.

So why couldn't he shake the feeling that they were being watched?

When they reached Jade's house, she dug into her jacket pocket for her front door key. As she turned the key in the lock, she suddenly turned around, nervous.

"You won't say anything to my mum about

this, will you? She ... she doesn't know that Dad talks to me."

"Don't worry, we won't say a word," Theo replied immediately.

At Jade's contemplative look, Theo realized that he shouldn't have jumped in quite so quickly. He'd done it again.

"Come on, then," Jade said. And she opened her front door.

Theo had a last quick look around. He could see nothing and no one out of the ordinary. But then what did he expect? Someone walking along, holding a placard saying, 'Yes, you're right! I *am* following you!' A dark car cruised past them, but apart from that, Jade's street was empty.

The first thing that hit Theo as he stepped into Jade's house, was the smell of air freshener and furniture polish and carpet cleaner and disinfectant. The smells were all mixed up together but distinct nevertheless and they made him want to sneeze. They all stood in the hall as Jade pulled off her jacket and hung it up on one of the coat hooks on the wall.

"Mum, I'm home," Jade called out.

A woman of about forty appeared immediately.

"It's raining. Don't leave your coat there, Jade. Put it in the bathroom until it dries. Otherwise it'll drip all over the carpet."

"It's only drizzling, Mum. My jacket barely got wet," Jade sighed.

"Jade, don't mess up the carpet," Jade's mum insisted.

With a deeper sigh, Jade removed her coat from the coat hook.

"OK, Mum," she said quietly. "I've brought some friends home. Is that all right?"

Mrs Driscoll looked Theo, Ricky and Angela up and down and from side to side. Theo could feel his face begin to burn. He tried to look straight back at Mrs Driscoll but it was hard. He felt like a germ being examined under a microscope.

"That's fine," Mrs Driscoll said at last. "As long as they take off their shoes."

"Mum, please!" Jade protested.

Theo, Ricky and Angela glanced at each other. Was this woman serious? Did she really want them to take off their shoes before they took another step into her house? One look at her face and Theo had his answer. Mrs Driscoll was totally, completely and utterly serious.

"I won't have them tracking mud through the house, Jade," Mrs Driscoll said firmly.

"We've been walking on the pavement," Jade said. "We were nowhere near any mud."

Mrs Driscoll glared at Jade.

"OK, Mum. OK," Jade said quickly. She turned to Theo, Angela and Ricky, a pleading look on her face.

"Would you mind? Please." Her smile was an embarrassed entreaty.

"Shame!" Angela muttered under her breath.

Mrs Driscoll didn't hear it, but Jade did. She chewed on her bottom lip. She was deeply embarrassed and doing her best to hide it from both her mum and her class-mates. Theo sure was glad it wasn't his mum who carried on like that. He would never live it down. If his mum did carry on like that, he'd never invite anyone to his house. Never, never, never. Jade must've been desperate to invite them round knowing what her mother was like. Theo had to admit that he was even more intrigued now to find out what was going on.

He bent down to untie his shoe laces. Angela bent down to do the same with her trainers. Ricky kicked off his shoes, which were slip-ons.

"Would you all like something to eat and drink?" asked Mrs Driscoll. "I could get you some orange juice or some cola and some sandwiches."

Theo didn't know about the others but he didn't want to take anything from Mrs Driscoll. She'd probably have her plates industrially cleaned afterwards.

"No, thank you," Theo replied.

Ricky and Angela mumbled the same.

"Mum, can we use the computer?" Jade asked.

"The computer?" Mrs Driscoll's voice was as sharp as a razor. "No. No, you can't."

And just like that, it looked like they were going to be scuppered before they'd even started.

# 9. Evidence

"Please, Mum. I'll be very careful – I promise," Jade replied quickly.

"Jade, you know I don't like you…"

"I'll be really, *really* careful," Jade continued. "And Ricky, Theo and Angela will be with me all the time so nothing will go wrong."

Mrs Driscoll took another look at her daughter's companions. "Jade…"

"Please? *Please*?"

"OK, then." Mrs Driscoll's voice was tiny. "But ten minutes only."

"Thanks, Mum." Jade smiled.

Mrs Driscoll still didn't look happy about it. Her eyes clouded over and her lips turned down. She looked like she was about to change her mind.

"I'll be extra careful, I promise." Jade smiled.

"I'll rinse off these shoes and put them out in the conservatory." Mrs Driscoll sniffed. She walked away with their shoes, holding them at arm's length, her head tilted backwards. Jade waited until her mum had left the hall, before turning to the others.

"Mum just … Mum…" Jade's expression took on a stubborn turn. She pressed her lips together and looked defiantly at all of them.

"All mothers are embarrassing," Ricky said easily. "Whenever anyone comes over to our house to visit, my mum breaks out the old photo albums and shows off my photos from the time I was born. I'm surprised she didn't keep one of my old, smelly nappies to show as well."

Jade laughed.

"You were going to show us something?" Angela prompted.

"This way." Jade opened the door to the room immediately to their left. It was shrouded in darkness, even though it was still light outside. Theo and his friends stood uncertainly at the door.

"Just a sec." Jade moved across the room and opened the heavy, dark blue velvet curtains.

It looked better with the curtains drawn, Theo thought. His first, second and third impressions of the room were that it was very cold and uninviting. The walls were a pale blue, the curtains and carpet were navy. Now that Jade had opened the curtains, dust motes swirled in the air like pirouetting dancers. There was a fine layer of dust over most of the furniture. Theo couldn't understand it. With Mrs Driscoll around, Theo would've thought that dust didn't stand a chance. Against the opposite wall, below the window, was a PC. A printer and a modem sat on a large, wooden table and beneath the table, Theo could see the processor, standing up on its base.

"I'll just switch it on." Jade pressed the POWER button on the processor. Immediately the monitor on the table crackled into life. Jade switched on the modem and the printer.

"What has the computer got to do with

your dad talking to you?" Angela asked.

Jade slid the PC mouse over its mat, clicking with deft movements as she selected the options she wanted.

"Take a look at this," she said at last.

Theo, Ricky and Angela gathered around the PC for a closer look.

<Page 1 of 2>
To: JDriscoll@JDriscoll.private.uk
From: PDriscoll@PDriscoll.private.uk

Darling Jade,

How are you? I know these messages frighten you – and that's the last thing I want. Please don't be scared. I'd never do anything to hurt you – or make you unhappy. I've tried to talk to you before but you couldn't see me. I want you to know that I'm watching over you. I wouldn't let anything or anyone harm you.

This is so bizarre. When I was alive, I was the last one to believe in life after life and here I am clinging on to

God knows what and God knows why. No, that's not strictly true. I think I know why I haven't moved up or on or over or whatever the phrase is. It's because I left some unfinished business behind me. Yes, that's a good way to put it – unfinished business. But that's my problem. Or maybe not... Jade, maybe you could help

Theo leaned forward to press the page-down <PG DN> key, but Jade hit the <ESCAPE> key to clear the screen before the second part of the message could appear.

"This is just one of the messages I've received," Jade said quickly. "I've had quite a few."

"Is this really from your dad?" Theo asked what they were all thinking.

Jade nodded. "At first I didn't believe it either, but it is him. He's said things in some of the other messages I've received that only he would know."

"What sort of things?" Angela asked.

Jade shrugged, careful to avoid catching

anyone's eye. "Different things. For example, two years ago when we were on holiday, Dad and I went out water-skiing. Mum wouldn't give it a try, so it was just me and Dad and the man driving the boat. Well, one of Dad's messages to me told me what the two of us were talking about. There's no way anyone else would have known that. And there've been lots of examples like that."

"What's this unfinished business your dad talks about?" Ricky asked softly.

Jade licked her lips. For the first time she looked at them directly. "I … nothing. It's not important."

"Are you sure about that?" Ricky prompted.

"Positive."

"If you were that positive, I don't think we'd be here," Ricky pointed out. "You can't expect us to help you if you only give us half of the story."

"There isn't much more to tell." Jade's voice held angry defiance. "I just needed to tell someone what was going on, that's all. I just needed to know that I'm not imagining things or going crazy."

"Well, we all saw a message..." Theo began.

"But that doesn't mean it's from Jade's dad," Angela cut in. "That message could've been sent by anyone."

"But I just told you that Dad mentioned things..."

"But he could've told someone else about your holiday without you knowing it," said Angela. "He might've told someone he worked with all about your holiday and they could be the one sending you all these messages."

"Why would anyone want to do that?" Theo asked.

"How should I know?" Angela said, exasperated. "All I'm saying is that there are a number of other options to consider before we start believing that Jade's dad is talking to her from beyond the grave and via the Internet!"

"Why is it so hard for you to believe in ghosts?" Ricky frowned. "Don't you believe in something above and beyond us?"

"No, I don't," Angela said, her voice crackling with bitterness. "We're alone in this world and when you die, you die. That's it. End of story."

Theo didn't need to ask. He knew she was thinking about her brother, Tom. Angela's voice always grew cold and hard when she thought about Tom. Theo knew it was just a defence mechanism. Angela's way of trying to stop herself from hurting too much but from her voice, it didn't seem to do much good. Impatient, Ricky turned from Angela to Jade.

"Jade, has your dad asked you to do anything for him?" Ricky asked.

"I … not really, no."

"What does that mean? Not really?"

Licking her lips, Jade's expression finally cleared. She had obviously made a decision about something.

"I want all of you to promise that you'll never talk to anyone about what I'm about to show you."

"We've already promised," Theo reminded her.

"I want you to promise again," Jade insisted.

"We promise." Ricky answered for all of them. "You can trust us, Jade. I promise you that too."

Finally satisfied, Jade turned back to the screen and recalled her last message. Hitting the <PG DN> key, she stepped aside to let Ricky, Angela and Theo read the rest of the message.

<page 2 of 2>

But that's my problem. Or maybe not... Jade, maybe you could help me. It would be so wonderful to rest. Simply to rest. I wouldn't even mind if that was all there was to it. I'm so tired. And existing like this ... it's worse than you can possibly imagine. It's like being stuck in a box with no way out. It's like being stuck in a coffin. This world has become my coffin, Jade. But you could help me to change all that. I did something very wrong and I need your help to put it right. Don't worry, it's not illegal or dangerous. I just need you to deliver something for me. Once this package is delivered I will be at peace. Just saying the word makes me long for it. Let me know when you've found it and I'll give you more instructions. I'm getting weak. Time to go. I know you'll help me. I know I can rely on you.

Dad.

"What package?" Angela asked immediately.

Theo raised his eyebrows. Ricky sighed. Theo found himself wishing that for once, Angela wouldn't be quite so direct, quite so blunt. He and Ricky could put up with it because they knew that Angela wasn't as brusque as she sometimes came across but it did tend to put other people's backs up – like now!

"I don't know." Jade's voice was clipped. "I wish I did. Dad hasn't said."

"Your dad wouldn't have asked you to deliver this package unless he thought you knew what he was talking about." Angela frowned.

Jade bristled like a porcupine. "Angela..."

"Angela, if Jade says she doesn't know then she doesn't," Theo interrupted quickly.

"I only…" Angela trailed off. "Sorry, Jade. Sometimes I get a bit … sorry!"

Jade visibly relaxed. "Sometimes I get a bit … myself!" A trace of a smile flickered across her face.

"Have you spoken to your mum about this?" Ricky asked.

"Not yet. To be honest, I don't think I will."

"And you haven't spoken to anyone but us about it?" Ricky questioned.

Jade shook her head.

"What exactly did your dad do?" said Ricky.

"He worked for Diadem-21 Software Systems. He's the one who thought up and designed *The Land of Dreams* – amongst others."

"I thought he worked with Theo's mum in the marketing department," said Angela.

"I didn't know *The Land of Dreams* was your dad's idea." Ricky was astounded. "Theo never told me that."

"I didn't know," Theo replied, more than a little impressed himself. "Jade, I knew your dad was a software engineer but I didn't realize he was responsible for *The Land of Dreams*."

"What's *The Land of Dreams* when it's at home?" Angela frowned.

Ricky stared at her. "Where have you been? It's the latest PC game. You have to solve puzzles and defeat the cyborgs and live through your worst nightmares. It's great! It starts when you go to bed and then you find yourself in the middle of a strange, gruesome dream but you can't wake up and then..."

"I get the idea, Ricky," Angela interrupted.

"That was all Dad's idea," Jade said proudly.

"The only game that comes anywhere near *The Land of Dreams* is *Dyna-Cybo Warriors*!" Theo told Angela.

"Sounds like a classic!" Angela said wryly.

"It is!" Theo enthused.

"Dad's friend, Alex came up with that one – *Dyna-Cybo Warriors*," said Jade. "I don't think Dad was too happy about it to be honest. He always refused to mention it and I think he and Alex had a big quarrel about it."

"Over what?"

Jade shrugged. "I don't know all the details. All I know is Alex stopped coming over to our house after the game came out."

"Was your dad jealous?" Angela asked what Theo was wondering.

"Of course not," Jade denied vehemently.

"Did your dad and this Alex person stop being friends just because Alex came up with a game as good as *The Land of Dreams*?" said Angela.

"My dad's not like that. I don't know if that was the reason – and neither do you," Jade replied, chips of ice glinting in her eyes.

Angela shrugged. "I was only saying."

"Some things you should keep to yourself." Jade's feathers were definitely ruffled.

"Jade, you should've said about your dad," Theo said. "That's amazing. What other games…?"

"Theo!" Angela interrupted.

"Sorry!"

"Your dad and Alex … what a thing to fall out over. A game," Ricky said thoughtfully. "Huh! Grown-ups!"

"That's just what Mum said, except she said

'Men!' instead of 'Grown-ups!'" said Jade.

"So when you two are grown-up men, you'll have no chance!" Angela grinned.

Ricky looked at Theo. "I think we're being got at!"

"You're not grown-up men yet!" Angela scoffed. "You've got more brains than most grown-up men!"

"That was a good backhanded compliment." Jade looked at Angela, impressed.

Theo was tempted, but he didn't reply. From the look on her face, Angela was remembering her brother and the rest of his so-called friends. They were the ones responsible for Ricky being kidnapped and now they were all in prison.

"Jade, why...?" But Ricky got no further.

"That's enough. Jade, switch off the computer. That's enough." Mrs Driscoll stood in the doorway, swaying slightly. It was as if she wanted to come further into the room but just couldn't bring herself to do it.

"Mum, can't we just...?"

"No. Switch it off – NOW." Mrs Driscoll ordered.

Jade and her mum stood watching each other. Long moments passed. Finally Jade did as directed and switched off the PC.

"I think you others should go home now. I'm sure your parents must be wondering where you've got to," Mrs Driscoll said.

*Why doesn't she just lift us up and hurl us out the door? She's not even subtle*, Theo thought sourly.

They all stood up and left the room, skirting around Mrs Driscoll who stood at the door like a sentinel. Theo remembered reading a Greek myth once about a scary three-headed, dragon-tailed dog called Cerberus who guarded the gates to Hades, but that dog had nothing on Jade's mum!

"See you tomorrow, Jade." Ricky smiled.

"Bye."

"Yeah! Bye!"

Mrs Driscoll followed them out into the hall. Ricky had opened the front door before he remembered.

"Mrs Driscoll, can we have our shoes back please?"

Startled, Mrs Driscoll glanced down at

their feet.

"Just a moment." Mrs Driscoll disappeared towards the back of the house. Moments later she returned carrying a tray lined with newspaper. And on the newspaper sat Theo's, Angela's and Ricky's now cleaned shoes.

"Thank you," Theo mumbled as he retrieved his shoes. He didn't wait to lace them up either. Mrs Driscoll made him feel too uncomfortable. The moment his shoes were on his feet, he was out the door. And Angela and Ricky weren't far behind him either. Jade stood at the front door, her eyes dancing with what she couldn't say now that her mum was right behind her.

"I'll see you at school tomorrow," Jade said at last.

"Take care, Jade." Ricky smiled. "And thanks for showing us your computer."

"No problem," Jade replied.

But Theo watched her face as she shut the door. "No problem" was an out and out lie. Jade had problems up to her eyebrows - only one of which was her dead father.

## 10. Uncle Pascoe

"So what d'you make of that then?" Angela asked as they walked along.

Theo shrugged. "I'm not sure what to think."

"Jade doesn't behave like someone whose dad has just died," Angela said, more to herself than to anyone else.

"How's she meant to behave?" Ricky rounded on her. "Where's it written that you have to behave in a particular way? And besides which her dad died two months ago."

"Two months isn't very long. Two months is nothing..." Theo began.

"Ricky, I was just saying," Angela said defensively. "There's no need to jump down my throat. It's just that when she talks about her dad, there's no *sadness* there."

"I think she's feels sad when she *thinks* about him," Theo said slowly. "When she talks about him though it's like ... it's like..."

"It's like he hasn't really gone," Ricky finished. "And he hasn't, not if he's sending her messages."

"D'you really believe those messages were from Jade's dad?" Angela asked, incredulously.

"I don't know. I think so."

"You don't sound too sure."

"What makes you so sure they *aren't*?" Ricky asked.

"Well, it's a horrible idea for a start." Angela wrinkled up her nose. "I mean, the thought of anyone getting messages from their dead dad. But over the *Internet*? Why didn't he just visit her in her house and haunt her like normal ghosts do?"

"Using the Internet was the only way he could communicate with her. He said so," Theo reminded the others.

"I don't understand you two." Angela stopped walking and eyed Theo and Ricky speculatively. "Ricky, it's like you're falling over backwards to believe every word that Jade says to you. And you Theo, you're ready to believe Jade on the evidence of a couple of mail messages which could've been sent by anyone."

"I never said I believed Jade," Ricky replied evenly. "But I'm prepared to believe her."

"What does that mean?"

"It means that whether or not the messages are from Jade's dad - *she* believes they are and that's what's important," said Ricky.

They all carried on walking as Angela and Theo thought about what Ricky had said.

"I've had an idea." Angela grinned suddenly. "Why don't we use Bullet's new program to see whether or not the messages are genuine?"

"What program?" asked Ricky.

"Angela, what on earth are you on about? Bullet's program is designed to solve crimes, not check out the source of information on the Internet," Theo pointed out.

"What program?"

"But if someone is trying to trick Jade or pull a fast one then maybe Bullet's program will help us find out what's really happening..."

"WHAT PROGRAM?"

"All right, Ricky! All right! Don't get your boxers in a bunch!" said Theo. "Bullet's written a program to solve crimes – so he reckons."

"If he says his program solves crimes, then it does," said Angela, stung.

Theo gave her a knowing, smug look. "You have got it bad, haven't you?"

Angela's face turned an immediate and deep shade of scarlet.

Amazed, Ricky stared at Theo. "You're joking. Not Bullet! Come on!"

"I know. I thought she had more taste, but it seems her taste is all in her mouth!" Theo laughed.

Ricky joined in, with his deep, throaty laugh that could probably be heard three streets away.

"Both of you – get stuffed!" Angela flounced off in high dudgeon.

"Oh come on, Angela," said Theo, still laughing. "We're only teasing."

"I don't fancy him. It's a lie."

"Yeah right!" Ricky grinned. "Careful you don't trip over your nose, Pinocchio!"

"If you two don't stop, I'll never speak to you again." Angela fumed.

"Not another word." Theo tried to suppress his laugh.

Ricky mimed zipping up his lip. Theo joined in and mimed turning a key against his mouth.

"Don't overdo it!" Angela sniffed.

Which set Ricky and Theo off again. And only seconds passed before Angela creased up laughing too.

"Excuse me? Do you three go to St Christopher's School?"

Startled, Theo turned to look at the man who'd spoken to them. He was a man in his mid to late twenties, with wavy, dark brown hair and sparkling, merry brown eyes. He smiled at them and unlike most grown-up smiles, this one seemed genuine. Even so, Theo eyed him warily.

"Do you three go to St Christopher's School?" the man asked again.

Theo nodded.

"Do you know a girl called Jade Driscoll?"

No one spoke.

"I'm trying to get in touch with a girl called Jade Driscoll?"

"I'm not being funny, mister, but we've been told not to talk to strangers," Ricky said suspiciously.

"I quite understand," the man nodded. "These days you can't be too careful. My name is Pascoe DeMille. Jade's my god-daughter. I know her father, Paul, but I've been abroad for the last five and a half years and we've kind of lost touch. In his last letter, Paul said they were hoping to move to a new house and that he was hoping to send Jade to St Christopher's after her primary school. I was hoping to find someone who knew Jade so that I could find out where Paul and his wife, Laura and Jade live now."

Theo, Ricky and Jade looked at each other – each one waiting for someone else to speak.

"I'm sorry Mr DeMille, but Jade's dad died two months ago," Theo said at last.

Pascoe stared at Theo, profoundly shocked. "No… Don't say that. He didn't."

"I'm sorry," Theo replied, uncomfortably. He turned to Angela and Ricky for help.

They weren't going to leave all this to him, were they? But the look on their faces said otherwise. Their eyes danced away from his as they looked at the sky, the houses – anywhere but at Theo and Pascoe DeMille.

"Jade and her mother, Laura – are they all right? Do they need anything? Someone should've let me know..." Pascoe was distraught. He turned away from Theo, as if to hide his face.

"Someone should've let me know," Theo heard him whisper.

Theo felt sorry for the man. He looked devastated. Theo wondered how he'd feel if he suddenly heard that Ricky had died. How long would it take him to get over it – if he ever did?

"Stop it!" Theo muttered sternly to himself. He didn't like the direction his thoughts were travelling in. Ricky wasn't going to die. Only old people died.

Pascoe turned to face them, his expression so sad and weary that Theo caught his breath.

"Do you know where Jade lives? I'd like to see her and her mother."

"I … I'm sorry but I don't think we should give out Jade's address just like that. I'm not being funny but we don't know you…" Ricky said uncomfortably.

"I understand. And you're right of course," said Pascoe. "In that case could you tell Jade that her Uncle Pascoe is in town and was asking for her. Her mum and dad have had some letters from me over the years so she'll know who I am. If you could ask her to phone me at the Bishop's Arms Bed and Breakfast Hotel. That's where I'm staying."

Ricky nodded. "We'll tell her at school first thing tomorrow morning."

"Thank you. I'd appreciate it," Pascoe replied. "I'd be very grateful if you could ask Jade to contact me and not tell her mum I'm here until I've had a chance to speak to her."

No one replied.

"I know it's rather a strange request but … well, Laura and I didn't exactly part on very good terms. I'd love to see her again of course, but I think I'd better speak to Jade first and make sure of my welcome."

"Oh, I see. OK." Theo nodded.

"Thank you for your help," Pascoe said sadly. And he walked slowly away from them.

"You were right not to give out Jade's address," said Angela, once Pascoe was out of earshot. "You don't know him from Adam. He could be anybody."

"Not from the look on his face when I told him about Jade's dad. He was genuinely upset," said Theo.

"He could've put that on..." Angela began.

"Pardon?" Theo couldn't believe his ears.

"He could've been acting."

"For goodness' sake, he's Jade's godfather," Theo reminded Angela.

"So he says – but you only have his word for that."

"True," Ricky agreed.

Theo shook his head. "Don't you two trust anyone?"

"I trust you," Ricky said without hesitation.

"So do I," Angela agreed. "But not many other people. And certainly not that man. I mean, Pascoe DeMille? That doesn't sound like a real name for a start. He might be the guy who's sending Jade all those email messages."

"Why?" asked Theo.

"I don't know," Angela said impatiently. "All I'm saying is you're too quick to believe every word anyone says to you."

"And you're too fast to mistrust and disbelieve everything you're told," Theo countered.

"So between the two of you, you get it about right," Ricky soothed, as if he could smell there was a full scale argument coming.

"So what do we do now?" Theo asked, calming down.

"I think first thing tomorrow morning we should grab Bullet and get him to help us," Angela suggested.

"You can grab him if you want to. Me? I'll keep my hands to myself," Theo sniffed.

Ricky laughed, adding, "We must get Jade to trust us. I reckon we still don't have the full story."

"We can't force Jade to confide in us if she doesn't want to," said Angela.

"We won't have to force her. I'll charm her," Ricky grinned.

Angela and Theo looked at each other.

"Poor thing," Angela muttered under her breath.

Theo looked from Angela to Ricky and back. "I don't know who I feel most sorry for," he said. "Bullet or Jade."

## 11. Tricks and Lies

"Where've you been?"

Theo skidded to a halt next to Ricky, who stood outside the school gates. He'd run practically all the way from his house and his blood was now roaring in his ears, his knees were aching and he was beginning to get a stitch. He pulled his rucksack back up on to his shoulder where it had been slipping down his arm.

"Sorry, Ricky. I overslept." Theo bent at the waist and panted to try and get his breath back.

"And where's Angela?" Ricky frowned.

"How should I know?" Theo replied testily.

"She was meant to be here at least thirty

minutes before the school buzzer," said Ricky.

"Take it up with her, not me." Theo straightened up.

"Am I going to have to do all this by myself?"

"I'm here, aren't I? Stop nagging. You sound like my mother."

Ricky and Theo glared at each other. The expressions on their faces eased and they each gave a rueful smile.

"Good morning, Theo. How are you this morning?"

"I'm fine, Ricky. What about you?"

"I'm fine. Lovely weather we're having!"

"They did say we might get some rain later!"

Ricky grinned. "I don't suppose you've seen Angela?" he asked in his politest voice.

"I'm afraid not," Theo answered.

"What a shame!"

"Can't be helped," Theo laughed. "So what's the plan?"

"Let's go and see Bullet and later when Jade arrives we'll tell her that her godfather is looking for her," said Ricky.

"Is Bullet here already?" Theo raised his eyebrows.

"Are you kidding? Bullet's the first to arrive and the last to leave. You know how he loves computers."

"I thought he had one at home," said Theo.

"He does, but his mum and dad have limited him to only one hour on the computer a day."

"How d'you know?"

Ricky tapped the side of his nose. "I have ways of finding out these things."

Theo considered. "You asked him when he arrived this morning – right?"

"Right!" Ricky admitted. "A nice bit of deduction on your part!"

"Take notes! I'll make a detective of you yet!" Theo laughed.

"Come on. Let's go and see exactly what Bullet's new program does."

Theo and Ricky walked into the school.

Once they were in the computer room, Ricky plonked himself down on the chair next to Bullet, before pulling it right up to Bullet's computer screen.

Theo looked around the room. Apart from Bullet and now themselves, it was empty. But even though it was empty there was still the whirr of the fans in each processor case to break the silence. Theo sat down on the other side of Bullet, enjoying the emptiness and peace in the room but he knew it wouldn't last long. It wouldn't be long now before the room started to fill up.

"Hi Bullet! How's it going?" Ricky grinned.

"Er … I … I'm fine. How're you?" Bullet smiled. He looked nervous but not particularly puzzled.

He's not surprised to see us, Theo realized.

"Angela warned you we were going to – what was the word she used? – grab you?" said Ricky.

"She did say something about it," Bullet admitted.

"When did you see her?" Theo asked.

"Last night. She came round to ask if I could help her with her computer homework."

Ricky and Theo leaned back in their chairs and made faces behind Bullet's back. So much for the element of surprise. Angela really did have it bad!

"So, is it true? Have you really written a program to solve crimes?" asked Ricky.

Bullet nodded, looking suitably modest yet proud of himself.

"Does it work?" Theo asked bluntly.

Bullet's smile of pleasure faded slightly. "Well, I've only tested it out on one real, proper crime so far."

"What crime was that?" asked Theo.

"The one where Ricky was kidnapped," Bullet explained.

All at once, Ricky and Theo became very still.

"And of course that was a slightly different case, because one of you had all the facts and knew what was going on, but..."

"Did Angela tell you about that?" Ricky asked quietly.

Bullet nodded.

"I see," Ricky replied quietly.

"So as I was saying, one of you had all the facts – but of course you two didn't ... know t-that at ... the ... time..." Bullet's voice trailed off altogether.

Bullet looked at Ricky, then Theo and back again. He might've been a bit slow when it came to people, but even he could detect the tense undercurrent now flowing through the room.

"I'm sorry. I know I'm not meant to mention it but I thought it would be OK with you two … as you know all about it … I'm sorry…"

"You used what happened to me to test your program?" Ricky asked.

Theo wasn't fooled by Ricky's soft, even tone for a second. Ricky was a hair's breadth away from going nuclear. And Theo couldn't blame him. He glared at Bullet, willing him to shut up. Couldn't he see what he was doing? Every time he opened his mouth it was only to change feet. Theo hadn't seen Ricky so *furious* in a long, long time.

"Oh yes! I inputted all the data about your kidnapping," Bullet began eagerly. "And my program didn't do too badly. As I said, it's not quite the kind of case that I'd designed my program to solve but…"

"I'm sorry my getting kidnapped wasn't quite the kind of case you had in mind." Ricky's voice dripped ice.

"I … I … didn't mean it like that. I mean … I know it must've been horrible for you," Bullet said, flustered.

"Horrible. Yes, it was … horrible," Ricky repeated, his body tensed up like an over-tightened spring.

"I … I…" Bullet looked horror-stricken as he spluttered his way through another apology. It didn't help that Ricky's expression was now thunderous.

Ricky stood up, the better to glower down at Bullet. Bullet was in real trouble. Ricky was just about to lose it.

"Ricky…" Theo warned off his friend. "Come on, Ricky. Calm down."

Ricky took a deep breath and his body relaxed visibly. He took another deep breath and slowly sat back down in his chair.

"Sorry Bullet, but what happened to me was more than just some test data for your program," he said at last.

"I understand that." Bullet nodded at once.

"And I hope you don't mind that Angela told me about it."

"If I did mind, it's a bit tough and two-thirds now, isn't it?" Ricky pointed out.

"I promise, it'll go no further," Bullet said.

"So you were saying about your program?" Theo reminded him, feeling it was time to change the subject.

"Oh yes!" Bullet exhaled gratefully. "When I tested it on the information Angela gave me, the program said that I should get more information from the person who set up the dare game that led to Ricky being kidnapped in the first place – so it was spot on there. It knew that Angela had more information than she was initially letting on."

"And what does your program tell you about Jade?" Ricky asked.

"Well, I don't have enough information yet." Bullet shook his head.

"What information do you need?" said Ricky.

"What've you got?" Bullet replied.

"How much has Angela told you?" asked Theo.

"Just that someone claiming to be Jade's dad sends her email messages and he wants her to deliver a package," said Bullet.

"Do *you* believe in ghosts?" asked Ricky.

"Oh please," Theo said hastily. "Let's not start all that again."

The last thing he wanted to do was get into another discussion about ghosts. After sleeping on it, he was beginning to wonder if maybe Angela's point of view on this was closer to the truth than Ricky's.

"We haven't got much more information than what you've been told already," Ricky said.

"I'm brilliant but even I'm not a miracle worker!" sniffed Bullet. "I'll need more data than that. Besides, I don't see that a crime has been committed and my program is meant to solve crimes, not mysteries."

"What crimes *does* your program solve?" asked Theo.

Bullet leaned forward towards the keyboard. Theo realized that he'd been just waiting to be asked!

BULLET'S CRIMEBUSTER PROGRAM

Select crime to be solved:

1. Murder
2. Kidnapping
3. Theft (Stealing)
4. Fraud (Lying)
5. Bullying - verbal
6. Bullying - physical
7. School-related Crimes

Enter number: ________

"That looks dead impressive and seven-eighths," Theo couldn't help but admit. "Does it work? Does it really do all that?"

"Of course it does," Bullet said with indignation. "Or at least, I've written all the programs. Now I've just got to get some real cases with proper data to test the programs and make sure they work."

Theo studied the screen again. "Couldn't we input the data we already have?"

"Under what heading?" Ricky frowned.

"I was just about to ask that," said Bullet.

"How about fraud or lying – number 4?" suggested Theo.

"Who's lying?"

"And about what?"

"Jade's dad. Or at least the person who's sending Jade all those email messages and claiming to be Jade's dad," Theo said.

"You don't know that." Ricky's frown deepened.

"You don't honestly think that Jade's dad is really sending her messages?"

"I thought Angela was the one with the closed mind, not you," Ricky countered.

"I don't call it having a closed mind. I call it having a brain," said Theo.

"Hang on a minute..."

"Why don't I try number four and see what the program comes up with?" Bullet interrupted. "It can't hurt."

Theo sat back in his chair. Ricky leaned forward. Theo frowned. He couldn't understand it. Usually he and Ricky never argued – about anything. And yet they had blown up at each other twice in as many days. What was going on? They'd had disagreements before, but never like this. Never so … personal. It was as if the very subject of ghosts was stirring up all kinds of nasty things. Not ghosts and ghouls and things that went bump in the night. But it was forcing Theo to think about death and dying and things he didn't want to think about. Dying was for old people, but his mum and dad were old. And deep down, Theo knew it wasn't just old people who died. Young people died too… Suddenly, Theo didn't want to do this any more. They were getting into very murky waters here. He didn't want to be forced to think about Jade and her dad. That road led to too many other places that he had no desire or intention of exploring.

BULLET'S CRIMEBUSTER PROGRAM

FRAUD:

Select type of fraud:

1. Fraud involving money

2. Fraud involving jewellery or other possessions
3. Computer fraud
4. Cons and tricks
5. Other

Enter number: ________

"That menu is about as much use as a chocolate teapot," Theo said impatiently.

"Why d'you say that?" Bullet asked.

"Your menu selections are all too vague. I mean, in Jade's case numbers two, three or four or all of them could apply," Theo replied.

"You have to pick the one that's most likely to apply," Bullet said. He was obviously miffed that Theo had found fault with his program.

"OK. How about number four?" Theo suggested.

"Cons and tricks? You really think so?" Ricky asked.

Theo nodded.

"Cons and tricks it is then." Bullet inputted the number four.

Immediately a series of random numbers and letters scrolled down the screen. Theo sat back, immensely disappointed.

"I thought I'd fixed that bug," Bullet muttered to himself.

"So much for computer power," Theo said with disgust. "We'll just have to use our brains and do it ourselves."

"I'll have it fixed by this afternoon," Bullet protested.

"We're not going to hang about waiting for you to fix your program," said Theo.

"Let me know anything new you come up with and I'll input that data into my program. I'm sure it'll help you," said Bullet.

Ricky stood up. "Come on, Theo." He smiled sympathetically at Bullet. "Thanks anyway."

"I will get it working. I will. You wait and see," Bullet insisted.

Ricky and Theo left the room. Mrs Daltry ambled down the corridor deep in convers-ation with Mr Dove. Mrs Daltry had a liquorice allsort in her hand, on its way to her mouth. She stopped abruptly when she spotted Ricky and Theo and made a great show of rubbing her eyes.

"A paranormal event in itself. You two are here *early*! Whatever next?"

Ricky grinned. "We're here to help Bullet with one of his programs."

"Does he need help?" Mrs Daltry asked, surprised.

"Yep! And in more ways than one," Theo said, sourly.

"I heard that!" Bullet called out from the computer room.

Theo couldn't help but smile in Bullet's direction. Bullet wasn't too bad. Maybe he was a bit of a computer nut but he was willing to help them. All things considered, Bullet was OK!

"If the two of you are looking for something to do, you can help me and Mr Dove set out the equipment for the first lesson," Mrs Daltry suggested.

"That would be great," said Mr Dove. "It would give me a chance to get to know you better. Mrs Daltry has told me a lot about you."

"Actually, we were just on our way to the library, weren't we, Theo?" Ricky said with haste.

"Er … yes, that's right. We have some research to do."

"Hhmm!" Mrs Daltry didn't sound too convinced but she let it pass. "All right then, but just make sure you do go to the library and don't dawdle in the corridors."

Theo and Ricky scampered off, eager to get away from the teachers before Mrs Daltry insisted on their help.

"So where are we going?" Theo asked, once they were out of Mrs Daltry's earshot.

"To the library, like I said."

"Why?" Theo asked, surprised.

"I've had an idea. I think I know how we can make sure that it's really Jade's dad trying to communicate with her."

"Oh yes? I'm all ears."

"The first thing we need to do is track down the host machine that he's using to send Jade those messages," said Ricky.

"That information usually comes with the text of the message itself, but I can't remember seeing that in any of the emails that Jade showed us."

"Yes, I know. We'll have to ask Jade if we can see the messages again." Ricky pushed open the library door and headed straight for the non-fiction/computing section. This section was over by one of the large library windows and the cold October morning sunlight streamed in, illuminating the books.

"I thought we could..." Ricky stopped abruptly when he saw who had beaten them to it. It was Jade.

Ricky made a bee-line over towards Jade, a grin splitting his face from ear to ear. Jade stood watching his approach, her face a mask. Theo felt a strange uh-oh warning chill creep down his spine. Something in Jade's deliberate lack of expression warned him to watch out.

"Hi Jade," Ricky enthused. "I think we've come up with a way to help you find out for certain whether or not your dad is really sending those messages..."

"He isn't," Jade said. Her voice was soft, but the tone was firm enough to stop Ricky in his tracks.

"Pardon?"

"I said dad didn't send me those messages. I made them up."

A long silence followed.

Ricky frowned. "I don't understand."

"OK, then. Here it is in words of one syllable. It was just a wind-up. I sent those messages to myself." Jade turned to Theo. "You were right after all, Theo. I was just pulling your leg."

"Why?" Theo asked, his eyes narrowed.

"Why not? I didn't have anything better to do and you two and Angela were obviously looking for something to get you going. So I gave you something. It was your ad about your detective agency that gave me the idea."

"I don't believe you." Ricky's voice was ice-cold.

Jade shrugged. "Suit yourself. But my dad's d-dead. How can he send me Internet messages?"

"But we saw the messages..." Ricky began.

"I typed those in myself. I thought it would be a good joke, but I want to stop it now before it goes any further."

"Why?" asked Theo.

Jade looked confused. "Why what?"

Theo regarded her steadily. "Why stop it now? You could've had a lot more fun watching us chase around trying to find out what was going on. So why stop now?"

"I … I…" Jade got no further. As unexpected as it was shocking, Jade's face crumpled up and she burst into tears.

"Just leave me alone," she sobbed. And she tried to run past them out of the library.

"Jade, what's going on?" Theo stepped in front of Jade to block her escape. "You didn't make it all up. I don't believe that for a second."

"Why?" Jade asked bitterly. "You were convinced I was lying before. Why the sudden rush to believe me now?"

Theo couldn't answer. He didn't know how to answer.

"You didn't make up those messages, did you?" Ricky asked. There was more than just a question in his voice. A hope against disappointment was mingled in there as well.

"Yes, I did," Jade said quickly. "You won't get me to say anything else."

"Jade, you can trust us. I promise you," Ricky said earnestly. "We won't let you down."

Jade looked around fearfully. Theo did the same, wondering what Jade was looking for. They were quite alone in the library, so why was she so afraid?

"Don't you understand?" Jade's voice was no more than a desperate whisper. "Dad told me not to talk to you or anyone. He told me that if I do, he won't be able to talk to me ever again. He'll just wander around this earth, unable to rest. Well, I'm not going to do that to him. And I can't lose him again. I won't. *I won't.*"

Jade ran around a now stunned Theo and in seconds she was out of the room. Theo and Ricky regarded each other. Theo didn't like the way things were going – not one little bit. He didn't like the way an icy chill was slowly invading his body, atom by atom.

"If it really is Jade's dad sending her messages," Ricky began, "why did he tell her not to talk to anyone about him? I mean, why would he *care*?"

"That's just what I was thinking. Surely he wouldn't mind that Jade had told us. It can't make any difference to him," said Theo. "D'you know what else I think?"

"What?"

"I think there's something very kippery going on here. I think Jade's in danger."

## 12. Watching

"So what now, Robin?" Ricky frowned.

"Excuse me but I'm Batman. You're Robin," Theo argued.

"Yeah, OK. But what now?"

"We're going to have to catch up with Jade and convince her to trust us," Theo decided. "If we can't do that, then there's not a lot more we can do for her."

"We haven't done anything," Ricky said with sudden anger. "She needs our help and we haven't done a thing. And I'll tell you something else, if anything happens to her, I'll never forgive myself. Never."

"Ricky, aren't you taking all this a bit too seriously?" asked Theo. At Ricky's scowl, he added hastily. "I mean, our detective agency was only meant…"

"Our detective agency? This has nothing to do with our detective agency," Ricky said, incensed. "Jade's in trouble. *Real* trouble – whichever way you look at it."

"You're remembering when you were in trouble, aren't you?" said Theo.

Silence. Then Ricky nodded.

Theo sighed inwardly. He wasn't sure when this had stopped being just a joke, a bit of fun. Maybe it never was. But one thing was for sure. It was deadly serious now. Ricky would make sure it was treated no other way.

"Let's go and find Jade," said Ricky.

"What about the information you wanted to look up?"

"That can wait. Finding Jade is more important." Ricky was out of the library before the sentence was over.

Theo ran after him. Ricky was so determined to help Jade, even when she told them she didn't want their help. Theo sensed that part of it was because of Ricky's own experiences when he'd been kidnapped but there was more to it than that. Theo ran down the corridor, only a couple of steps behind his friend.

"Where're we going?" Theo puffed.

"Right here. All the girls come in here when they want to be alone or have a cry – I bet."

It was the girls' toilets. Theo eyed them with distaste. He didn't want to stop here. The boys always passed this part of the corridor in a hurry. And what if someone should see them parked outside the girls' loos? They'd have a mountain of explaining to do. And an even larger mountain of teasing to put up with. Theo shifted uncomfortably from foot to foot.

"You don't know she's in there."

"No, but it's a good place to start." Ricky knocked on the door. "Jade? Jade, are you in there? It's Ricky."

He put his ear to the door. Silence.

"Jade, I know you're in there." Ricky turned to Theo and shrugged. He didn't know if Jade was in there or not but he wasn't going to give up now. "I'm not going away until you come out."

Still nothing.

"If you don't come out, then I'm coming in," Ricky warned through the door.

The silence around them deepened. Ricky gathered himself up to his full height. He turned to Theo again. "Come on, Theo."

Theo's eyes widened. He shook his head slowly. "No way! No way am I going in there!"

"Oh come on. There's nothing to be afraid of," Ricky cajoled.

"Ricky, you're my best mate and I'd do anything for you, but I'm not going in there," Theo said, adamant. "The only way you'll get me over that threshold is to knock me out first and drag me in."

"All right then. I'll go in by myself. You keep watch." And without another moment's hesitation Ricky walked into the girls' toilets.

Theo couldn't believe it. His admiration for Ricky shot through the roof. There was no place his friend wouldn't go. No place his friend was afraid of. But mostly Theo felt that Ricky had lost his mind! The girls' toilets! Nervously, Theo looked up and down the corridor, praying that he wouldn't see anyone he knew. And if there was anyone else besides Jade in the girls' loos then it would be all around the school in two seconds flat that Ricky went in there.

Suddenly there came an indignant shriek and Ricky came flying out of the toilets, followed by Jade.

"Ricky Burridge, just what d'you think you're doing?" Jade stormed.

"I did say I'd come in if you didn't come out."

"Yes, but I didn't think you meant it," Jade ranted. "Are you nuts?"

"Probably." Ricky grinned. "But we couldn't let you leave just like that. We want to help you."

"Whether I want you to or not – right?" Jade wiped her damp cheeks with the back of her hand.

Ricky grinned. "Something like that."

Jade studied Ricky as if she'd never seen him before. And Ricky didn't flinch, didn't back away. He stood his ground and looked straight back at Jade.

"You're persistent, aren't you?" Jade smiled reluctantly.

"I think the word you're looking for is stubborn," Theo chipped in.

Ricky grinned. Jade's smile faded to nothing.

"Look, please don't think I don't appreciate what you're trying to do for me. I do. It's just that, I lost Dad once and now he's come back. I couldn't bear to lose him again. Talking to him now, even though it's only by computer, well, it's … it's like he never died."

Theo licked his lips nervously. All kinds of responses flashed through his head but he bit back every one of them.

"Why did your dad tell you not to talk to us?" Ricky asked.

Jade shook her head. "I'm not supposed to tell you. I've said too much already. If Dad's watching me now, he might decide to stop sending me messages for not doing as he asked."

"But in that earlier message you showed us, your dad said he could only communicate via email messages on the PC," Ricky pointed out.

"He meant that's the only way he could talk

to me. That doesn't mean that he's not standing right next to you now," said Jade.

Both Ricky's and Theo's heads whipped round. The corridor was empty. Or was it...? Theo felt an icy knot tighten in the pit of his stomach. The whole idea gave him goose-bumps. What if Jade's dad was right here, watching them? Why, the whole seemingly-empty corridor could be crawling with ghosts! Theo nervously looked around. Now that the thought had entered his head he couldn't get it out again.

"Mr Driscoll, if you are here, I want you to know that Theo and I only want to help," Ricky said loudly, his voice totally serious. "We wouldn't do anything to upset Jade. Honest we wouldn't."

The silence of the corridor echoed back at them. Even Jade looked nervous.

"Didn't your dad like you talking to your friends when he was alive?" Theo asked.

"Are you kidding? Dad loved to meet my friends. He always encouraged me to bring my friends home. He always said the more the merrier."

"So why would he change his mind now?" Ricky said gently. "I don't think people change so much when they're dead."

"He might've done. Maybe dying does things to you."

Theo had to fight down the strongest urge to laugh – more with unease than with humour – or to waggle his fingers in his ears or crawl away and hide under a table somewhere. He'd never taken part in such a bizarre conversation. Ricky and Jade were seriously discussing whether or not dying would change a person, apart from in the most obvious way. They were really wondering if it could change your character.

"So what exactly did your dad say in his last message?" Ricky prompted.

Jade looked uncertain, then her expression cleared. "I'll show you."

They all walked together to the computer room. Without a word, Jade sat in front of one of the computers, whilst Theo and Ricky pulled up a chair on either side of her.

"What're you all doing?" Bullet asked from the other side of the room.

"Nothing," Ricky said tersely.

"Can I watch?" Bullet asked.

"No." All three of them spoke in unison.

"OK!" Bullet replied cheerfully and he carried on with what he was doing.

With deft fingers, Jade signed on to her Internet account and went through the directory of her email messages.

"Have you told anyone else about your dad trying to contact you?" Ricky whispered.

Jade shook her head.

"What about your uncle?" Theo remembered.

"What uncle?"

"Your Uncle Pascoe. We saw him yesterday. He told us to tell you he's staying at the … the Bishop's Arms bed and breakfast hotel."

"My Uncle Pascoe? What're you talking about? I don't have an Uncle Pascoe," Jade said, confused.

"He said he's your godfather but he's been away. He … he didn't know about your dad. When we told him he was really upset. He wanted your address…"

"You didn't tell him…"

"Of course not," Theo denied.

"I'll have to ask my mum about him, but I certainly don't remember him." Jade frowned. "Uncle Pascoe...? That doesn't ring a bell at all."

She turned slowly back to the screen and selected the last message listed.

To: JDriscoll@JDriscoll.private.uk
From: PDriscoll@PDriscoll.private.uk

Darling Jade,

I saw you and three of your friends go into our house yesterday. I hope you didn't tell them about me. I hope you didn't show them the messages I've been sending you. No one must know about me but you. I won't be able to talk to you any more if you tell others about me. Don't even tell your mum. She wouldn't understand. No one understands except you. Have you found my package yet? I need it desperately. Don't stop searching until you find it. Time is running out.

And remember, not a word to anyone – or you'll never hear from me again. Remember, I'm watching.

Dad.

Ricky and Theo studied the message carefully.

"Now d'you see why you mustn't become involved. You'll scare Dad away if you do. I've got to sort this out for myself," Jade whispered.

*I saw you and three of your friends go into our house yesterday...*

Theo's blood turned to ice-water. Yesterday, as they entered Jade's house, Theo had had the uneasy feeling that someone, somewhere was watching them. And now his worst suspicions were being confirmed. They *were* being watched.

Theo swallowed hard and clenched his fists, and forced himself to calm down.

"Hang on! Your dad mentioned a package in one of the other emails we saw." Ricky frowned. "Didn't he say something about delivering it once you'd found it?"

"That's right," Jade replied reluctantly.

"What package was he talking about?" Theo asked.

"I don't know. I still haven't found it yet."

"Do you know where or who you're meant to deliver the package to?" said Theo.

Jade didn't answer.

"Did your dad go into more details about the package in one of his other emails? Maybe in one of the messages that you didn't show us?" asked Ricky.

Jade looked away, chewing on her bottom lip.

"Jade…"

"No, Theo," Ricky interrupted. "Jade has to make up her own mind once and for all about us. We can't push her."

Anxiously, Theo watched Jade. Ricky was right. They couldn't stop now. It wouldn't be right. Theo wanted to find out what was going on just as much as Ricky did. But it was up to Jade now.

What would she decide?

## 13. A Dirty, Rotten Trick

"OK. But you must do what I say with no arguments," Jade said at last.

"No problem."

"Agreed."

"And you can't change your mind or withhold information or anything like that," Ricky added. "We're going to see this through till the end."

The end. What would that be, Theo wondered. And how would they recognize it? Was it simply a case of finding this mysterious package and delivering it? Would Jade's dad really go away and rest in peace once the package had reached its final destination? Somehow, Theo didn't think it would be that simple.

"I guess the first thing I should tell you is ... I think I found the package this morning," said Jade.

"What was it?" Theo asked eagerly.

Just at that moment, Angela came through the door. "Sorry, I'm late. What's going on?" Angela headed straight for them.

"Can we tell her?" Ricky asked carefully.

Jade considered, then nodded. Ricky beckoned Angela closer. For once, Bullet's computer screen did not have one hundred per cent of his attention.

"Jade thinks she's found the package that her dad wanted her to find," Ricky whispered.

"Oh? What was it then?" Angela asked.

They all turned to Jade, waiting for the answer.

Jade dug deep into her coat pocket. "I think Dad is after this." She took out a small, brown, padded envelope with "Private" written across it in sloping writing.

"Is that your dad's handwriting? Can you be sure?"

"What's in it?"

"Have you opened it yet?"

The questions came thick and fast. Jade looked slightly overwhelmed.

"Yes, it is my dad's writing. Yes, I am sure. And I don't know what's in it 'cause I haven't opened it yet," Jade shot back before gulping for breath.

"Well? What're you waiting for?" Angela asked impatiently.

Ricky shook his head. Theo sighed. Angela was at it again! But to everyone's surprise, Jade burst out laughing.

"Angela, I never used to like you – but I do now!" Jade smiled.

"Oh, thanks!" Angela raised her eyebrows.

"I didn't mean that the way it came out," Jade said quickly. She paused. "Actually, I think I did!"

"Oh, thanks!" Angela said again.

Angela and Jade smiled at each other and where they weren't particular friends before, they were friends now.

"I was wondering whether or not I should open the envelope," said Jade. "But I think I'll follow Angela's advice."

"Are you sure?" Ricky asked.

"No." Jade shook her head after a long pause, "But I'm going to do it anyway."

She tore open the envelope immediately, as if she wanted to do it before she could possibly change her mind, and peered in. Her eyes widened in surprise. Theo thought the suspense would kill him. He longed to just snatch the envelope from Jade and take a look for himself but he had to wait. Jade turned the envelope over and shook the contents out into her hand. It was an unlabelled CD in a clear plastic case, and a black floppy disk.

"Is that it?" Angela asked.

Jade took another look in the envelope, then nodded.

"I wonder why your dad was so desperate for you to find those and deliver them," Angela mused out loud.

"Let's have a look and see what's on them," Ricky suggested.

"D'you think we should? I mean, I don't want Dad to … to get upset with me."

"I don't see why he'd get upset with you just because we're trying to help," said Ricky carefully.

"It seems to me that you need all the help you can get," Theo added.

"Your dad should be glad that you're not alone in this, that your friends are prepared to do what they can to help sort this out," said Angela.

"I suppose so." Jade didn't sound totally convinced.

She looked around and gave a half-hearted smile. Angela was right about that at least. She didn't want to go through all this alone. She looked at Theo, Ricky and Angela in turn, her gaze speculative. She was surprised at all of them, but especially Ricky. He seemed almost desperate to help her. She remembered that he'd been in serious trouble himself a while ago. She didn't know too much about it – Ricky had refused to speak about it and Theo had warned everyone off who was even a little bit curious. Was that it? Did Ricky think she was in a similar situation to him and that's why he was so keen to help? If that was it then he had got hold of totally the wrong end of the stick.

Jade still remembered the howl of anguish

that had erupted from her when her mum had told her about her dad. She had refused to believe it, as if not believing it would somehow change the fact that her dad had died. And then the weeks and weeks of anger. Anger at her mum, anger at her dad, anger at the world. Anger that she had buried deep within as she turned in on herself, terrified to let out what she was really feeling. She wouldn't go back to that again. At least this way, she had something, some small part of her dad to talk to.

And if she was right about Ricky's motives for helping her, what about the others? What was in it for them?

"Why are you all doing this?" Jade couldn't help asking.

"Doing what? Helping you?" asked Theo.

"This isn't just so you can have a case for your new detective agency?" Jade asked suspiciously.

"This has nothing to do with Theo's idea about starting a detective agency and you know it," Ricky said calmly. "Stop trying to push us away. It won't work."

Silence. Then Jade smiled. "So which disk should I try first?" she asked.

"The floppy." Ricky decided at once.

Jade pushed the floppy disk into the disk drive and pulled her chair closer to the keyboard. "I'll see what's on the disk first before I do anything else."

They all watched as Jade typed.

```
>DIR A:

> LOST~1.PGM
  LOST~2.PGM
  LOST~3.PGM
  ATLANT.PGM
  ATLAN~1.PGM
  ATLAN~2.PGM
  DIARY.EXE
  INSTALL.EXE
  SETUP.EXE
```

"What are those files then?" Bullet's voice came out of nowhere, making everyone jump.

"Bullet, this *is* private," Theo pointed out.

"That's OK. I'm not about to tell anyone,

am I?" Bullet said cheerfully. "And besides, I reckon Jade needs my help. I'm the computer expert in this room."

"And modest with it," Theo muttered.

"I don't believe in false modesty," Bullet replied with a beaming smile. "So what're all those files then?"

"Look, more and more people seem to be getting involved in this," Jade said firmly. "I want everyone in this room to promise that it won't go any further. I'll tell you four and that's it. No more."

"We promise," everyone said immediately.

"All right then," Jade said. "To answer your question Bullet, I don't know what these files are."

"Step aside then." Bullet elbowed his way to the computer and stood over Jade like a vulture, waiting for her to stand up. Eyebrows raised, Jade got to her feet.

"Let me try and install it. That seems like a good place to start," said Bullet.

Everyone watched avidly as Bullet ran the INSTALL program. The message <PLEASE WAIT> flashed up on the screen.

"Whilst we're waiting for that, I'll let Dad know that I think I've found what he's been asking for," said Jade.

Jade moved to the next screen and started up her Internet account using her name and password.

"Don't tell him that you're trying to find out what's on the disk though," Theo warned.

"Don't worry. I wasn't going to," Jade replied.

To: PDriscoll@PDriscoll.private.uk
From: JDriscoll@JDriscoll.private.uk

Dear Dad,

How are you? I think I've finally found what you're looking for. I'm sorry it took so long but I was looking for a big parcel rather than a small, padded envelope. The envelope has two computer disks in it – a CD-ROM and a floppy disk. Is this what you were after? If so, what should I do next? Will I be able to see you? Please let me know. I'd love to see you. I wouldn't be frightened – honest. I'm at school, but I'll wait around in the computer room for a while in case you're able to reply to this message immediately.

Love,

Jade.

Jade clicked on the <SEND> button before standing up. She joined the others to see how far Bullet had got.

"It's asking me to insert the CD-ROM disk now." Bullet explained the self-evident message on the screen.

"Go on then," Angela prompted eagerly.

Bullet inserted the CD-ROM into its drive and pressed the <ENTER> key as directed. All at once, it was as if the hard disk drive went crazy. It spun and clicked and whirred in a frenzy.

"These disks don't have a virus on them, do they?" Bullet asked worried.

"How should I know?" Jade replied.

"I think I should have run the virus checking software first." Bullet's eyebrows knitted together with anxiety.

"Mrs Sumonu is going to hit the roof if you've introduced a virus on to one of her precious computers," Ricky pointed out unhelpfully.

"I should definitely have run the virus checking software," Bullet muttered. "Mrs Sumonu is always saying that if we bring disks in from outside, we must make sure they're clean first."

"I'm sure it'll be OK." Theo said doubtfully.

"At least this is a standalone computer," Bullet said. "We should be grateful for that."

"Bullet, you're so clever! What does that mean – standalone computer?" Angela asked.

Theo shook his head as he watched Angela. The tone of her voice and the expression on her face conjured up a single word in his mind – simpering!

"It means that if Jade's disks do contain a virus, at least it won't be passed down the school network to all the other computers in the room," Bullet explained. "The three machines on this side of the room haven't been connected up to the school network yet."

"I really don't like the sound of that." Theo pointed to the processor casing.

The disk drive sounded like it was revving up to take off into orbit. Then all at once, the noise stopped. Bullet watched the screen, waiting for some clue as to what just happened.

"It wants a password now to continue." Bullet frowned.

They all turned to Jade, expectantly.

"Don't look at me. You all know as much as I do now." Jade shook her head.

"What was your dad's name?" asked Bullet.

"Not was. *Is.*" Jade corrected, firmly. "His name *is* Paul."

No one spoke. Theo shifted uncomfortably in his seat. Jade really didn't believe that her dad was dead. And thinking about it, if her dad could still talk to her, if he could still communicate, then surely he wasn't really dead – not in the real sense of the word. Theo wasn't sure what to think any more. Death and dying and being dead were subjects he didn't like to think about. They were taboo subjects and as soon as they entered his head, he always pushed them out again. It was as if just to think about them was to invite them in to do their damage. Theo didn't want that. And try as he might, he just couldn't get comfortable around Jade when she talked about her father. Truth to tell, he was afraid that the death of her dad might somehow be ... contagious.

"I'll type your dad's name in as the password," Bullet suggested. "Although I'd be really surprised if your dad had chosen anything as obvious as that."

He hadn't. A warning message flashed on the screen.

INVALID PASSWORD. 1 OF 3. PLEASE TRY AGAIN.

"Bullet, what does that mean? 1 of 3?" Angela asked.

"I'm not sure," Bullet said slowly. "I'll try another password."

"Which one this time?" asked Ricky.

"I'll try Jade's name," said Bullet.

And although he could type using all ten fingers, Bullet typed in J-A-D-E using only his index finger to ensure that every keystroke was correct.

INVALID PASSWORD. 2 OF 3. PLEASE TRY AGAIN.

"I thought so." Bullet withdrew his fingers from the keyboard as if it had suddenly turned white hot.

"You thought what?" Ricky questioned.

"I've got one more chance to get the password right," Bullet replied.

"And if you don't get it right?"

"The best that will happen is the installation program will just stop," said Bullet.

"And the worst?" Theo didn't want to, but he had to ask.

"It depends on how malicious the installation program is," Bullet replied. "It can be anything from wiping out the directory it was being installed into, to erasing the whole hard disk."

"It can't do that ... can it?" Ricky asked aghast.

"Easily," Bullet said grimly.

"But that hard disk has got lots of people's classwork and homework on it," said Ricky.

"I know. We won't be too popular if the disk gets wiped."

"No kidding," Theo scoffed. "Now tell us something we don't know."

"Maybe we should quit while we're ahead?" Angela suggested.

"But we can't give up now. You all said you'd help me. You're not going to give up at the first hurdle, are you?" Jade protested.

"We can still do this. I'll backup the hard disk first, just as a safety precaution. Then we can try re-installing the software on your dad's disks again," said Bullet.

"Go on then," Jade agreed reluctantly.

Bullet hit the <ESCAPE> key. Nothing happened. He pressed it again. Then pressed it simultaneously with the <CTRL> key. Still nothing happened. Bullet's expression was stony as he tried <ALT> with the <F4> key, <CTRL> and <C> together and <CTRL> and <Y> together. But he was still in the installation program.

"If this doesn't work, we've got problems."

Bullet shook his head.

"Should we start panicking yet?" Ricky asked, eyebrows raised.

"Not yet," Bullet replied.

He tried holding down the <CTRL> <ALT> and <DEL> keys all at the same time.

WARNING: IF THE COMPUTER IS RESET AT THIS TIME, ALL DATA ON THE HARD DISK WILL BE ERASED. PLEASE ENTER THE INSTALLATION PASSWORD.

"I think you can start panicking now." Bullet slumped in his chair.

"So are you going to try another password then?" Jade asked.

The screen from which Jade had sent the email to her dad beeped loudly.

"Dad's replied to my message." Jade jumped out of her chair and moved over to the other screen.

Immediately everyone gathered around, watching avidly as Jade displayed the message on the screen.

* * *

To: JDriscoll@JDriscoll.private.uk
From: PDriscoll@PDriscoll.private.uk

Darling Jade,

Thank God! Thank God you've found my package at last. I was beginning to lose hope of you ever finding it. Yes, it's exactly what I've been waiting for. Here's what I want you to do. DON'T TRY TO READ THE DISKS! That's most important. After school, I want you to take them to the shopping centre. At exactly four-thirty, I want you to drop the package into the bin outside The Body Shop. Then you're to go home. I'll send you a message at exactly five o'clock – and I'll have a surprise for you, but only if you've followed my instructions to the letter. Remember, don't tell anyone about me and don't show my messages to anyone. I'll be watching you. All my love.

Dad.

* * *

"I don't know who's sending you those messages, but it's a dirty, rotten trick if you ask me." Bullet scowled.

Startled, Jade asked, "What d'you mean?"

Bullet was surprised. "Well, that obviously can't be your dad because he's been asking you for ages to find this mysterious package – but if it really was your dad, he'd have known where the package was from the beginning."

"He might've forgotten," Jade said quietly.

"Yeah right!" Bullet scoffed. "And even if he had forgotten *where* it was, he wouldn't have forgotten *what* it was. So why does he keep referring to it as 'the package' all the time? And since when does a ghost need a package to be dropped off in a bin outside The Body Shop? If your dad wanted to get rid of the package, he could've told you to throw it in the nearest bin in school or anywhere. And if he did want the package, surely he would've told you to put it on his grave or something? And what would a ghost want with a couple of disks? I reckon your dad must've been working on something really important and someone out there is trying to get their hands on it."

The room was as still as an early Sunday morning. You could've heard a feather drop.

Bullet looked around the room, confused. "I mean, that's what you all reckoned – right?"

Still no one spoke.

"I just thought it was a nasty trick." Bullet defended himself, even though he wasn't sure why. "Someone has obviously got hold of your dad's email account and password and they've been trying to get you to do their dirty work for them."

Theo looked down at the floor. If, at that moment his life depended on it, he still couldn't have looked at Jade. He, Angela and Ricky had each tried to tell Jade the same thing but she'd never listened. And in his heart, Theo could understand why. But now Bullet had come right out and hit the nail smack dab on the head. Bullet had come straight to the point where Theo and the others had danced gingerly around it. And truth to tell, Theo had begun to wonder if maybe, just maybe, the email messages might actually be from Jade's dad?

"It is a nasty trick, isn't it?" Jade's voice was barely more than a whisper.

Only now did Theo dare to glance up. Silent tears streamed down Jade's cheeks.

"I'm sorry. What did I say?" Bullet asked distraught. "*What did I say?*"

"Excuse me." Jade stood up and ran out of the room.

"Will someone please tell me what I said?" Bullet pleaded.

Ricky turned to him. "It's not your fault, Bullet. You only told her the truth, that's all."

"I don't understand."

"Jade believed those mail messages really were from her dad," said Theo.

Bullet's eyes widened like dinner plates. "You're joking."

Theo, Ricky and Angela all shook their heads.

"I wonder though," Angela said thoughtfully. "I wonder if Jade really did believe that those messages were from her dad? Or did she just want to believe it?"

"Does it make a difference?" Ricky asked.

"No, I guess it doesn't," Angela sighed.

"What about these disks?" Bullet asked. "What should I do with them?"

"Are you going to try and put in the password? You've got one more go left," said Ricky.

"Maybe we shouldn't fiddle about with the disks whilst Jade isn't here," Angela suggested.

"The best way for us to help her is to know what we're dealing with," Ricky argued.

"Any suggestion for the last password?" Bullet asked.

No one answered. Bullet shrugged.

"Does anyone know Jade's mum's name?"

"Laura." Theo remembered Pascoe DeMille mentioning it.

"OK then. Here goes nothing." Bullet took a deep breath and typed in L-A-U-R-A.

Immediately the disk drive sounded like it was winding up about to explode.

"What's happening?" Theo asked urgently.

"I think the program is wiping the hard disk," said Bullet. "I was afraid that would happen."

"Wiping the whole disk?" said Ricky.

Bullet nodded. "Mrs Sumonu is going to dance on our heads."

"Can't you just stop it?" Angela chipped in.

"That would probably make it worse not better. The best thing we can do is wait for the disk to be wiped clean and then to load everything on to it again," said Bullet.

"Can you do that without Mrs Sumonu finding out?" Theo asked.

"I can reload the operating system and all the software applications, but I can't reload everyone's work."

"Let's hope everyone who used this computer kept backups of their data." Ricky crossed his fingers.

"The trouble is," Bullet glanced down at his watch, "loading up the operating system and all the software will take at least two hours. Class starts in five minutes."

"We'll tell Mrs Sumonu we'll reload all the deleted software tonight after school," Theo suggested.

"No way," Ricky interjected. "We're going to put the disks in the bin outside The Body

Shop just as the mail message said. Tonight we're going to find out just who's doing this to Jade and why."

# 14. The Messenger

"Thank goodness for that. I thought this day would never end. We should head straight for the shopping centre," said Theo. "We need to plant these disks well before five o'clock. The person sending the messages needs to believe that Jade left them there."

"But suppose our 'messenger' is already there?" Angela said.

"We're going to have to take that chance," Ricky said.

Ricky looked no happier about it than Angela but they didn't have much choice. They'd just have to play it according to the email message and watch each other's backs. School was over at long last and now they had some business to take care of. Theo just wished his stomach would quieten down.

"You're … you're the ones I spoke to yesterday, aren't you?"

Theo jumped. And he wasn't the only one. They'd all turned the corner and there stood Pascoe DeMille.

"Er … yes, we gave Jade your message," Theo said hastily.

"What did she say?"

"She didn't recognize your name," Ricky said slowly. Theo could see the deepening suspicion in his friend's eyes.

"It's been a while since I saw her. I would've been more surprised if she had remembered me," Pascoe sighed. "Did you tell her where I'm staying?"

"Yes, we told her that as well," said Ricky.

"How is she doing?"

"Not too well." Angela chipped in before Ricky could answer.

Pascoe bent his head momentarily. When he looked up again, his eyes were shimmering with unshed tears. "I wish … I wish there was something I could do for her. Something I could do to make all this easier for her."

"Were you good friends with her dad then?" Ricky asked.

"I guess you could say that." The merest trace of a smile flickered across Pascoe's face. "We went our separate ways a while ago though. He disagreed with my choice of profession."

"Why? What do you do?" Angela asked straight out.

"I am … or rather I was an actor. Not a very good one. Not a very successful one. Paul told me I was wasting my time but…" Pascoe shrugged.

"Did you quarrel about it?"

"Angela!" Theo said, exasperated.

"I'm only asking." Angela defended herself.

"Yes, we did quarrel about it," Pascoe admitted.

"Jade's dad seemed to have quarrelled with a lot of people," Angela said. "He quarrelled with one of his friends at work about some game or another."

"Oh yes… *Dyna-Cybo Warriors*…" said Pascoe thoughtfully.

"How come you know about that?" Theo asked.

"Letters. We kept in touch."

"I thought you said you'd lost touch with each other," Ricky reminded Pascoe.

"Yes, we did."

All at once Theo didn't trust this guy – at all. Something didn't add up. And in the space of five seconds, he'd changed his story twice.

"D'you know Paul's friend, Alex?" Pascoe asked lightly.

Angela shook her head. Ricky and Theo didn't move.

"Well, Alex is a nasty piece of work. Take some advice, steer well clear. The only one Alex cares about is Alex," said Pascoe.

"How d'you know that?" asked Ricky.

"You'd be surprised." Pascoe stared at them without even blinking. His voice held an intensity that had Theo shifting back away from him. There was definitely something about Pascoe DeMille that was not quite right.

"You three take care of yourselves. And

remember to stick together," Pascoe said.

And with that he marched off past them and round the corner.

"What on earth was that all about? What did he mean by his last remark?" asked Angela.

"I have no idea. And did you have to volunteer quite so much information?" Theo rounded on Angela.

"What're you talking about? I barely spoke to the man," Angela said amazed. "What's the matter with you?"

"I don't trust that man. I think we should be careful of him. For all we know, he could be the one sending Jade those messages," said Theo.

"You'll be blaming it on the man in the moon next," said Angela.

"Don't you think he knew a lot of stuff for someone who lost touch with Jade's family years ago?" Theo suggested sardonically.

"I don't know. Maybe he's been catching up since we saw him yesterday," Angela said.

"Yeah, right! Oink! Flap! Oink! Flap!" Theo shook his head. Angela swung from not trusting anyone about anything to believing every word anyone said to her. It gave Theo a headache. He wished she would choose one or the other and stick to it.

"Shouldn't we call the police or something?" Angela whispered.

"And tell them what?" asked Ricky. "That someone claiming to be the ghost of Jade's dad asked her to dump some disks outside a shop in the centre and we're waiting for him to pick them up?"

"Ricky, I think Angela's right. The last time we were in a situation like this, we almost left it too late before calling the police," Theo remembered.

Nervously, he looked around as he spoke. The shopping centre was busy and noisy, with people bustling here, there and everywhere. The smell of burgers and pizzas wafting down to them from the food hall made Theo feel slightly sick. The last time he had felt like this was when Ricky had been kidnapped and he and Angela were about to confront the kidnappers. A queasy, uneasy feeling plucked at his stomach like a vulture over meat.

"I wish Jade was here," Theo couldn't help saying. "We're doing this for her. It feels strange her not being here."

"All the more reason to make sure we don't fail," said Ricky. "Did you see her when her mum came to pick her up this afternoon? She couldn't stop crying."

"I don't think Bullet's ever going to forgive himself," Angela admonished. "You should've warned him before letting him say all those things about the messages Jade was getting."

"He didn't give us a chance." Theo defended himself and Ricky. "He just launched straight in."

"It wasn't his fault, it needed to be said. It's just a shame that Jade had to hear it that way," Ricky sighed.

"D'you think Jade is OK?" Angela said, concerned. "Maybe after this we should go to her house and make sure?"

"Her mum won't thank us," Theo pointed out.

"Is that going to stop us then?" asked Angela.

Theo smiled. "Nope!"

"I wonder if someone will come for the disks," said Ricky, glancing down at his watch. "We've been here for over an hour now and nothing's happened."

"I've got to go home soon. I told Mum I'd be home by six," said Theo.

"That's what I told Marian," said Angela, talking about her foster mum.

"I hope someone turns up soon. I'd like to take a good look at the person who's doing this to Jade."

"Who d'you think is responsible for all this?" Theo asked.

"I have no idea." Angela shrugged. "I did wonder if maybe this had something to do with Jade's dad's friend, Alex."

"Why him?"

"'Cause apart from Jade's mum and your mum, I don't know anyone else connected with Jade's dad," Angela admitted.

"We don't have a big list of suspects, do we?" Theo smiled, wryly.

"We don't need a big list of suspects. This isn't an Agatha Christie mystery," Ricky dismissed. "All we need to do is wait to see if someone picks up the package and take it from there."

"Shouldn't we separate?" Angela suggested.

They all considered.

"Maybe we'd better not?" Theo said uncertainly. "Just in case?"

Strange that Pascoe DeMille's words about staying together should crop up in his head at that moment.

"OK."

"Agreed."

"Time to keep our eyes open and our mouths shut," said Ricky. "We wouldn't want to miss Jade's package getting picked up."

"If it does get picked up," Angela pointed out.

"If we can see the person who picks it up," Theo added.

Ricky and Angela looked at him. "Well, you never know," Theo mumbled. "We might all be wrong. Maybe it is Jade's dad after all."

"I thought I was the one who believed in ghosts, not you," Ricky said, surprised.

"I'm trying to keep an open mind," said

Theo, loftily.

"But not wide open," Angela said with sarcasm.

"Shush!" Ricky admonished.

And they all shut up. The centre was full of late afternoon shoppers, laughing, smiling, scowling. Was one of them waiting to see if some disks were dropped into the bin outside The Body Shop? Or was someone else waiting...? For the life of him, Theo couldn't tell which worried him more – the watchful gaze of the living or the dead. So here he was with Ricky and Angela waiting for something to happen.

And then it did. But it wasn't what any of them had been expecting.

A tall woman with auburn hair and dressed in an expensive, brown business suit strode up to the bin and looked down into it. With a frown of distaste she rummaged through it, obviously searching for something specific. Then a Cheshire cat smirk spread slowly over her face. She picked up the envelope Jade had found with *Private* written on it and pushed it into the larger than average handbag over her shoulder. She took a quick look around, and marched back the way she came.

"Come on," Ricky hissed. "Let's follow her."

They ducked around the escalators where they were hiding and started weaving in and out of the people milling around them.

"We've got to keep up with her. We can't lose her now," Ricky urged.

The woman marched with a purpose, keeping a straight line down the middle of the shopping centre. Theo thought his heart would stop when all at once she turned and looked behind her. Theo, Angela and Ricky immediately stopped in their tracks and looked anywhere but at her. Angela smiled at Theo and said, "D'you fancy a McDonalds instead?"

"Nah! I'm not that hungry." Theo shook his head.

"It's OK. She's moving again," Ricky said after a moment.

"Phew! Fast thinking there, Angela," Theo smiled.

"We're not out of the woods yet," Angela

pointed out.

They continued after the mystery woman, until all at once Ricky broke into a run.

"Oh no! She's taking the lift. Hurry up!"

They all belted towards the lift the woman had just stepped into. Ricky reached it first, just as the doors were closing. He slipped in sideways, whilst Theo and Angela watched in horror as the doors shut in front of them.

"What do we do? What do we do?" Theo tried to quash the panic which was beginning to rage in his stomach.

"Press the button for the other lift. I'll watch to see where this one stops." Angela pointed to the floor indicators between the two lifts.

Theo pressed the button, willing the second lift to move down faster. "Come on! Come on!" He clenched his fists, fear and frustration fighting within him.

"First floor. Car park level one. Car park level two. The lift has stopped on car park level two." Angela pointed up at the lift indicator. "Now it's stopping at car park level three."

"So which floor do we go to?"

"Both of them. We'll start with car park level two first," said Angela.

"If they're on level three, we'll never find them that way. They'll be out of the car park and half way to Scotland before we've even finished searching level two."

"If you've got any better suggestions, now is the time to open your mouth," Angela fumed.

Theo knew she wasn't angry with him. She was worried about Ricky, just as he was. Suppose the woman in the lift with him realized that Ricky was on to her. Where was Ricky now? Was he safe? Theo remembered the last time Ricky was in trouble. He wasn't going to go through all that again. But a terrible sense of deja-vu swept over him.

At last the lift arrived. To both Angela and Theo's annoyance and intense frustration a woman pushing a pram got into the lift with them.

"Hurry up, Sam. I haven't got all day," the woman called out to the girl of four or five standing outside the lift.

And neither have we, Theo thought, glaring at the girl, and willing her to get in the lift.

"Samantha!" The woman yelled, exasperated. She turned to Angela and Theo, smiling apologetically.

"I want a doughnut! I *need* it!" Samantha burst into tears and turned around to trot down the centre after her doughnut.

"SAMANTHA!" The woman pushed the pram out of the lift and headed after her daughter.

"Thank goodness for that." Angela pressed the button for the second floor of the car park. Nothing happened. She pressed it again and kept her finger on it. The doors shut so slowly, it was as if they were doing it on purpose. At long last the lift started to move, but it moved upwards as if it was on great-granny pedal power.

"I could run up the stairs backwards faster than this," Theo complained.

Angela pressed the destination lift button over and over again. It didn't make any difference. The lift continued crawling upwards. Theo could've wept with frustration. Finally they reached the second floor of the car park. The moment the doors were a body width apart, Angela and Theo were out of there. The lift opened straight out into the car park which at this time of day was full of cars. A hollow kind of silence echoed at them from all directions. Theo turned his head this way and that, desperate for some sound, some noise, some clue as to what was happening.

Nothing. No tall woman in a brown suit. And no Ricky.

"Should I call out for him?" Angela whispered.

"We'd better not. We might make things worse rather than better," Theo decided.

"Then we'd better split up. Back here in ten minutes." And Angela was off.

"Angela, no. We should stay..." But Theo was talking to himself.

What should he do now? Catch up with Angela so that they could stay together or try and find Ricky by himself? They would cover more ground apart but Theo wasn't happy about it at all. After a glance down at his watch, he turned and headed in the opposite direction to Angela. He scanned left and right, right and left for Ricky, wondering if he should dismiss his own advice and call out for his friend. The car park was vast, with alcoves going off in all directions. When his mum and dad came here with him for the weekly shopping, they always complained about the way the car park was designed. Unless you were lucky enough to park near a lift or you had years of experience of hunting round the car park, you stood no chance of finding your car until you were old and grey. Theo didn't know what to do for the best. He broke into a jog, moving up and down between the aisles of cars.

Still nothing.

Theo glanced down at his watch again. The ten minutes were up. He'd go back to the lift and if Angela hadn't found Ricky either then Theo was going straight to the police. The sudden, sharp click of heels made Theo freeze. He ducked down behind the nearest vehicle and stealthily made his way from car to car towards the noise. He tried to peep his head up, but ducked it down again when he saw two people only metres away from him. One was the woman in brown from down in the shopping centre but the man had his back to Theo. Praying that they hadn't seen him, Theo wondered what he should do next. Eyeing the ground with distaste, he gritted his teeth and lay down flat to look under the adjacent cars. Two pairs of feet – a woman in brown shoes with high heels and a man in grey lace up shoes and dark socks with bright dayglo green stripes stood two cars away. Could he get a bit closer? Keeping low, Theo crept around the first car. He was beginning to differentiate between the soft voices.

"You stupid woman! Why didn't you check first?"

"I didn't want to draw attention to myself. It was bad enough having to go through the bin in the first place," the woman replied with low anger. "And don't call me stupid!"

"If the shoe fits!" said the man. "Couldn't you tell it wasn't the right CD?"

"How was I meant to tell that without a computer? Or was I meant to read the disk with my fingernail?"

"The great big label marked *The Muppets*

*CD-ROM* should have given you just a slight clue!"

"Don't talk to me like that. You wouldn't have got this far if it wasn't for me."

"And exactly how far is this far?" the man fumed. "As far as I can see we're right back where we started."

"Maybe Paul just mislabelled the CD to throw us off?"

"See for yourself," the man said, exasperated. "The floppy disk is right, but the CD-ROM is a Muppet game!"

Theo had to risk it. Slowly, oh so slowly he crept around behind the voices until he was behind the car they were standing next to. It was an olive green Rover with a licence plate showing it was this year's model. Theo straightened up just the merest fraction. He could see the profile of the woman but, frustratingly, the man still had his back to him. But now Theo could see they were using a laptop computer which was perched on top of a dark green Rover. If he could just get a tiny bit closer...

Theo's knee hit against the bumper of the

car and the noise was like a cannon going off. Theo ducked back down but it was too late. The voices stopped immediately. Theo could hear footsteps heading in his direction. His heart pounded, his blood roared in his ears, he was going to be sick.

Move! *Move!* he told himself, but his feet refused to listen. Swallowing down his terror, Theo jumped up and ran like a rabbit, too frightened even to look back. He could hear two sets of footsteps racing after him.

"Come back here," the man yelled belligerently.

"He heard us. He was listening," the woman raged.

Theo willed his legs to run faster. He ignored his lungs screaming for air and his heart ready to burst and the stitch in his side like a plunging knife. He ran and ran.

"No! In the car! Quick!" The man's voice yelled out behind him.

And still Theo didn't look back. It was only when he heard the footsteps retreating that he dared to slow down and even then he was half afraid it was a trick. He turned but there was no one behind him. Sure he was going to have a heart attack at any second, Theo stopped to catch his breath.

Why had they stopped chasing him? He was what seemed like kilometres away from the lift and there was no one around. Theo still couldn't believe that he'd been so clumsy, so stupid as to alert them to his presence. He was so busy watching them to make sure that they couldn't see him that he'd forgotten to pay attention to the back of the car. Maybe if they'd still been talking at the precise moment that his knee had hit the car bumper… But it was useless to think about that now. They had heard him and given chase but at least he was safe now. Only … why had they given up so easily? Why had they stopped chasing him?

And then, horrifyingly, Theo realized why they had stopped running after him. They had gone back to their car and now it was heading straight for him.

They were going to try and knock him over…

## 15. The Accident

Once again, Theo took off. One word played over and over again in his head. *RUN!* If he could just reach the lift. If he could just run fast enough... But he could hear the car behind him getting nearer and nearer. Its engine roared like a ravenous lion about to pounce and Theo knew it was only a few metres behind him now. They were really going to run him down...

"Theo, over here."

The voice came out of nowhere. Theo didn't stop to work out who had called him or to work out the exact location of the voice. He had to get away, that was all he knew. He turned on the run and veered towards the voice.

"This way! Get down! Quick!"

Theo barely registered the fact that it was Pascoe DeMille. All he had on his mind were the occupants of the car who were trying to catch up with him.

"Down!" Pascoe pushed Theo down beside a black Land Rover and then squatted down himself. Both crouching, they frog-hopped their way behind the Land Rover and behind several cars, before stopping. Pascoe placed a finger over his lips as the two of them listened for the approach of the green Rover.

"Where did he go?" The woman's voice rang out over the low, steady purr of the car engine.

"He can't have got far."

"We'd better go. We can't risk staying here any longer. Someone might see us."

"Never mind. I'll deal with Theo Mosley and Jade..."

Theo didn't hear any more as the car drove off. But he didn't want to hear any more. He'd heard enough. The man and the woman in the car knew his *name*... How did they know who he was? Theo could taste the fear in his mouth. It was as dry as feathers and burnt like acid.

Pascoe straightened up and dusted himself off. "I warned you to stick with your friends." He shook his head.

"How did you know we should stay together?" Theo stood up and eyed Pascoe warily.

"I'm psychic!" Pascoe smiled. "You'd better get back to the lift. Angela and Ricky are worrying about you."

"Hang on! Where did you come from? How come you're up here helping me?"

"Actually, I was up here loading my groceries into my car," Pascoe replied. "I saw what was going on and thought you needed some help, that's all. It really looked like they were trying to... Well, I'm sure they weren't..."

"I think they were," Theo argued. "Shouldn't we go to the police?"

"I'd rather not get involved in the police – if it's all the same to you."

"Why not?"

"I have my reasons," Pascoe said, evenly.

"How did you know we'd be up here? Have

you been following us? How did you know all this was going to happen?" Theo still couldn't get over the feeling that Pascoe's arrival had been a little too timely, his intervention a bit too convenient. Was Pascoe in on this with the woman in brown and the man with the stripy socks? And now that Theo was thinking a little more calmly, there was something about the man in the stripy socks that was familiar. If he could just put his finger on it...

"I'd better get back to my car," Pascoe said. "Just be careful, Theo – OK?"

"How d'you know my name?" Theo stepped back from Pascoe.

The more the man opened his mouth, the more Theo suspected that Pascoe DeMille was not everything he claimed to be.

"The man in the car that was chasing you mentioned a Theo Mosley. I just assumed it was you."

"Aren't you going to do something to help?" Theo tried. "That man said he was going to deal with Jade as well – not just me."

"Don't worry. He won't get the chance."

Pascoe's face was as hard as granite as he stared down the car park. Then he looked at Theo and his face relaxed into a smile. "Not with you and your friends on the job."

And with that, Pascoe headed off down the car park. Theo watched him for a few moments, a deep frown creasing the skin on either side of his mouth. Theo turned and made his way back to the lifts.

No! I can't just leave it there, he shook his head vehemently.

Pascoe had to do *something* – even if it was just telling the police what had happened. He couldn't be that ineffectual, even if he was a grown-up. Theo turned back, ready to argue with Pascoe.

But there was no sign of him.

Theo looked up and down the rows of cars, but Pascoe was nowhere to be seen. His frown deeper now, Theo ran back to the lifts. Angela and Ricky were just entering one of them as he ran up.

"Wait! Wait for me!"

"Theo! We were just about to go to the police."

"Where on earth have you been? We were worried sick."

"Where were *you* then?" Theo asked Ricky, annoyed.

"The woman rumbled me. When I didn't get out on this floor, she pressed the button for the next one up. And when I didn't get out there either, she pressed the button for the ground floor and accused me of playing about with the lifts. I had to get out on the ground floor and then she went up again," Ricky explained.

"So with all that wandering up and down the car park lifts, we must've just missed each other," added Angela.

"But never mind that," Ricky dismissed. "Theo, what happened to you?"

"Simple. The woman in brown met her accomplice – it was a man but I didn't see his face. Then they both heard me eavesdropping and tried to run me over with their car."

Ricky and Angela stared, but Theo's expression was too grim for this to be a joke.

"Are you all right?"

Theo nodded.

"Are you sure?"

"Yes."

"Let's go to the police. This is getting serious." Now Ricky's face was as grim as Theo's.

"That's not all," Theo added.

"I would've thought that was enough," Angela said, eyebrows raised.

"Guess who helped me get away from the two in the car?"

"Who?" Angela and Ricky asked in unison.

"Pascoe DeMille."

"Pascoe!" Angela was stunned. "What's he doing here?"

"Shopping – or so he said," Theo replied.

"Lucky he was here then," Ricky said slowly.

"Isn't it just?" Theo agreed.

Silent moments passed before anyone spoke.

"Hhmm … d'you think Pascoe is working with the other two or is he after the disks for himself?" asked Angela.

"I think he's working alone or for someone else we haven't come across yet," Theo said at last. "Otherwise why would he help me out?"

"Unless he's trying to lull you into a false sense of security?" Ricky suggested.

Theo shook his head. "I don't think so. I think he was genuinely helping me but maybe he knew that we'd made a copy of the floppy and substituted another CD-ROM for the real one."

"How would he know that?" Angela frowned.

"I don't know. I'm only guessing," Theo said impatiently. "All I do know is that it's too much of a coincidence that he should just appear like that."

"Mrs Daltry says that sometimes coincidences do happen," said Angela.

"Yes, but Mrs Daltry…" And then it hit Theo. He stared at his friends. His mouth dropped open and stayed open. He couldn't believe it. And yet … and yet he was sure he was right.

"What's the matter?" asked Ricky, concerned.

Theo shook his head. He must've made a mistake. He *must* have… It was ridiculous –

preposterous. And yet, the more he thought about it…

"Come on Theo, sick it up!" said Angela.

Should he or shouldn't he? Theo wondered if he should tell his friends of his discovery. What if he was wrong? The trouble was once he had said it, there was no turning back. So he had to be sure...

"Nothing. Never mind." Theo couldn't tell his friends about his revelation. They'd never believe him for a start. And suppose he *had* got it wrong? There'd be hell to pay. But he was so *sure* he was right…

"Don't tell us it's nothing when we can see from your face that that's a blatant lie," frowned Ricky. "What's up?"

Theo made a conscious effort to think of something else so that Ricky couldn't read his expression. He was surprised the name of the person he had in mind wasn't blazoned across his forehead.

Theo was convinced he knew who had tried to knock him over.

But knowing it and proving it were two different things. He'd just have to find a way to prove it first – and that meant setting a trap. It wouldn't be fair to get his friends involved until he was absolutely certain. Especially after everything Ricky and Angela had already been through.

Theo's heart began to thump a slow, fearful tattoo in his chest, as if it knew and was protesting his decision.

"It's OK." Theo attempted to smile. "I thought I recognized the woman in the brown suit, but I didn't."

"Oh, OK. Let's pop in and see Jade on our way home," Ricky suggested.

"Fair enough," Angela agreed.

Theo didn't speak. His mind was overwhelmed by the course of action he was contemplating. If he was wrong he would be in the worst trouble of his life. But if he was right… Not only would he be in trouble, he'd be in *danger*. Theo wondered if he should tell his friends of his suspicions. It'd be so much easier to have company on this. Theo sighed inwardly. He was being selfish. He'd make one hundred per cent certain first and then he'd tell them.

An unwelcome question formed in his mind and refused to budge. If and when he needed his friends' help, would he be in a position to get it?

# 16. The Secret

"Hello, Mrs Driscoll. May we speak to Jade please?"

Mrs Driscoll's look could've felled an elephant at ten paces. She was not pleased. Glancing down at her watch, she asked, "Do you have any idea what time it is?"

"A quarter to six," Ricky said. "We won't stay long. We all have to be home by six o'clock."

"Jade's been very upset. She's in her bedroom asleep and I don't want to disturb her."

"It's very important that we see her. We have some important news to tell her," Theo said earnestly.

Ricky and Angela glanced at Theo.

"I think it's rather late to be…"

"Mum, it's OK. Please can I talk to them?" Jade walked down the stairs and towards the door.

"Jade, I…"

"*Please*, Mum."

"Just five minutes then. Is that understood?"

Jade nodded. Mrs Driscoll glanced down at everyone's shoes.

"You can all stay in the hall but you're not to go into the front room or any of the other rooms," she sniffed.

And with that she went into the living-room.

It was obvious that Jade had been crying – and not just a little either. Her eyes were puffy and swollen and her mouth drooped like a wilting flower.

"Jade, I need to talk to you – in private."

It was hard to say who was more surprised – Jade or Angela and Ricky.

"Theo, what's going on?" Ricky frowned.

"It's OK. I just want to ask Jade something," said Theo.

"So why can't you ask it in front of us?" asked Angela.

"Because I can't. Please, just give me a minute," Theo pleaded.

Reluctantly, Angela and Ricky stepped back as Theo stepped forward.

"Ricky, what's Theo up to?" Angela asked, suspiciously.

"I have no idea," Ricky replied.

Ricky tried to keep the hurt out of his voice at Theo's lack of confidence in him. He wasn't sure that he was totally successful. Since when did Theo keep secrets from him? Didn't Theo trust him any more? Ricky just couldn't work it out. He leaned his head forward to try and hear what Theo and Jade were whispering but they were speaking too softly for him to make out more than the occasional word. Now Jade was shaking her head vehemently. Theo spoke more urgently than before. He was obviously trying to convince Jade of something, but she didn't look happy. Jade looked over in Ricky and Angela's direction and said something to Theo. Now it was his turn to shake his head.

Curiosity burnt through Ricky like acid. Why was Theo shutting him out? What had he done? Maybe Theo blamed him for the fact that they'd all been separated in the car park and Theo had been in danger. But Ricky would never have jumped in the lift with the woman in brown if he'd known what was going to happen. When Ricky had been kidnapped, Theo had saved his life, not to mention his sanity. For a long time afterwards, Theo was the only one he could talk to about the experience.

Ricky shook his head slowly, unhappy with the direction his thoughts were leading him. He just wished the sour feeling in the pit of his stomach would go away. If Theo didn't trust him any more, why didn't he just come out and say so? Jade and Theo walked back towards them.

"Why did you want to see me?" Jade asked Ricky and Angela.

"I don't know if Theo just told you this, but a woman tried to pick up the disks you found," said Ricky. He looked directly at Jade. He couldn't look at Theo. "We followed her up to the car park above the shopping centre, where she met another man but we lost them."

"What Ricky's trying to say is that we're not much further forward," said Angela.

Jade looked at Theo. "Theo seems to think we are."

"Any thoughts you'd care to share?" Angela asked with fake nonchalance.

"No," Theo said simply.

For once Angela had no reply.

"Oh Angela, before I forget, d'you have Bullet's home phone number?"

"Yes."

Theo waited for Angela to carry on but she didn't.

"Can I have it please?"

"Why?"

"'Cause I need to talk to him about something."

"What?"

"Angela..." Theo said, exasperated.

"OK, OK!" Reluctantly Angela gave Theo the number. Theo wrote it down on the back of his hand.

"Anyway, we'd better get going," said Theo to Jade. "We don't want to get you into trouble."

"It's all right," Jade shrugged.

Ricky and Angela were the first ones out of the front door. Theo turned back to Jade just before he stepped over the threshold.

"We're … we're sorry about what happened earlier today – about the things Bullet said. None of us meant to upset you."

At first Theo thought Jade wasn't going to answer. He winced as he realized he was just dragging painful memories to the foreground again. He was about to shut the door, when Jade stopped him.

"Theo, don't worry about it. I guess … I guess I had to hear it. I think deep down I knew that Dad … that Dad was gone. It's just that this was my chance, you see. It was my chance to say all the things to Dad that I never got to say when he was here. It was a way of holding on to him."

"I understand that," Theo smiled.

He leaned forward and whispered something in Jade's ear. She smiled, but it didn't last long. She regarded Theo and said, "Just be careful, OK?"

"Careful is my middle name," Theo grinned.

And with that he shut the door.

They all walked along in silence.

"You've become very secretive all of a sudden," said Angela.

Theo shrugged. It wasn't exactly as if he could deny it.

"Don't we get to hear what's going on then?" Ricky asked.

Theo looked at Ricky. Ricky was looking straight ahead. Theo sighed. He'd known at Jade's house that Ricky was upset with him. Theo wasn't the only one who had difficulty hiding his true feelings.

"Soon. I just have to check something first. OK?"

Ricky shrugged. Theo sighed again. Ricky was even more upset with him now, not that he'd ever say as much.

"Well, this is my street. I'd better get going before Mum breaks out the bloodhounds," said Theo lightly. "I'll see you both tomorrow."

"Yeah."

"Sure."

Angela and Ricky walked away without a backwards glance. Theo watched them go with a heavy heart. He longed to call them back and tell them exactly what was going on but he couldn't. He just couldn't. As he'd explained to Jade, this was something he was going to have to do all alone. And the thought of it terrified him.

## 17. To Catch a Thief

Ricky's face was thunderous as he watched Theo deep in conversation with Bullet and Jade. Last night was bad enough, but now Theo seemed to be rubbing Ricky's face in it. When Ricky had arrived at school that morning, Theo was standing by the school gates. Ricky had made the mistake of thinking Theo was waiting for him. Theo soon put him right.

"I'm not waiting for you. I'm waiting for someone else," Theo told him in no uncertain terms.

Theo hadn't exactly said, "Now get lost!" but it was there, in his tone of voice.

If Theo didn't want to be friends any more,

why didn't he have the courage to just come right out and say so? Why make it clear to everyone in the class that he and Ricky had fallen out, without telling Ricky how or why first? Ricky couldn't understand why Theo was doing it. In fact, Ricky would've said that Theo was the last person to behave like that.

"Good morning, everyone."

"Good morning, Mr Dove."

Everyone scooted back to their places.

"I'll be taking you for your double lesson this morning," Mr Dove smiled.

Theo looked out of the window. He sat up in surprise when he saw Pascoe DeMille standing in the school grounds, looking up at Theo's classroom window. Jade obviously hadn't been in touch with him yet. Pascoe spotted Theo and waved frantically. Theo turned to look at Jade who sat at the back of the class. She looked terrible. Theo wondered if she'd managed to get any sleep at all. As if she knew she was being watched, Jade turned to him. Her expression was sombre as she nodded to him before facing the front of the class again. Theo watched Mr Dove as he walked up and down the class handing out worksheets. Pascoe would just have to wait. Theo had more important things on his mind at the moment. He picked up his duffel bag and emptied its contents on to the table. Now where on earth had he put it?

"Hello, Theo," Mr Dove smiled as he searched for a free space to put Theo's worksheet on the table before him.

"Hello, sir," Theo replied.

"It looks like you've brought everything including the kitchen sink to school," Mr Dove said dryly.

"Sorry, sir."

"What're you looking for?" asked the teacher.

"My pen," explained Theo.

"It's right there in front of you," pointed the teacher.

"No, that one doesn't work," Theo said.

"Then why carry it around?" Mr Dove smiled.

Theo shrugged, embarrassed. He used his forearm to sweep everything back into his bag.

Mr Dove moved on.

"You can use one of my pens if you like," Ricky offered.

"No, it's OK," Theo declined.

Theo turned to talk to Bullet. "Bullet, can I borrow a pen and your ruler?"

"Oh? Oh! Er… yes, of course." Bullet handed it over.

"What's wrong with my ruler?" Ricky said quietly.

"I prefer Bullet's."

"Suit yourself."

"I will," said Theo.

"Theo, I just said no talking," Mr Dove frowned.

"Sorry, sir. I didn't hear you," Theo apologized.

"That's because you were too busy talking. I think you'd better stay behind at break and write me a page on why sometimes it's better to open your ears rather than your mouth."

Theo lowered his head. "Yes, sir." It certainly hadn't taken Mr Dove long to show his true colours.

Ricky frowned at the teacher. "But that's

not fair, sir. Theo was only asking for a pen and a ruler."

"Never mind, Ricky." Theo glared at his friend. "Leave it. You'll just make things worse."

"I'd listen to Theo if I were you – unless of course you'd like to join him at break time."

"No, he wouldn't," Theo answered for Ricky.

Ricky shut up – more because of the way Theo was glaring at him than because of anything the teacher said. There was no doubt about it. Somehow, in some way, Ricky had lost his best friend.

Theo looked out of the window again. Pascoe was still there staring up at the school. From across the school grounds, Theo could see Mr Appleyard striding purposefully towards him – and it didn't take Superman's super vision to see that Mr Appleyard was not pleased to find a stranger in the school. Theo scowled at Pascoe. The last thing he needed was for Mr Appleyard to get antagonized. If Pascoe wasn't careful, he'd blow all of Theo's carefully laid plans.

The rest of the double lesson passed without incident. It also passed without Theo and Ricky saying one word to each other – which was a first. At last the buzzer sounded. Ricky leapt up and crammed his work into his bag.

"Theo, I don't think we should sit together any more," Ricky said tonelessly.

There was no disguising the shock on Theo's face. Ricky frowned. Had he made a mistake? Maybe Theo did still want to be friends after all.

"Ricky, I..."

"Theo, up here please, where I can keep an eye on you," Mr Dove ordered.

Theo got his things together and after a brief, abject glance at Ricky, he moved to the front of the class. Theo watched, dejected, as the rest of the class trooped out to enjoy the morning break.

"Theo, sit down and get on with it, or are you waiting for an engraved invitation?"

Theo waited for Jade, the last one out of the classroom, to close the door behind her. He turned back to Mr Dove and eyed him speculatively.

"Theo, are you going to sit down or not?" Mr Dove was beginning to get cross now.

"I think not," Theo said at last.

"I beg your pardon?"

"I don't see why I should sit down for someone who tried to knock me over," Theo said simply.

Mr Dove stared at him. His mouth opened and closed like a drowning fish.

"And please don't insult my intelligence by denying it. I know it was you."

Mr Dove burst out laughing. "Theo, I take my hat off to you. In my time, I've heard some amazing excuses and accusations from children trying to get out of the work I set them, but this one is in a class of its own."

"I know it was you. I recognized your voice."

"Let me get this straight. You claim that someone almost accidentally knocked you over and you're blaming me?"

"First of all, it was no accident, you meant to do it. And second of all I recognized your voice."

"So you never saw the face of this person who came at you?"

"No, I didn't. But then you already knew that. You must've known there was no way I could see your face from the back of the car where I was hiding. And when you drove at me, the last thing I was going to do was stop and turn to get a good look at you."

"I haven't a clue what you're talking about, but maybe we should both go to the headmistress and get this sorted out." Mr Dove's voice was now winter ice. "You can tell her your accusation."

"I think that's a good idea," Theo agreed. "I'll tell her how I know it's you because you're wearing the same yeuky socks with the bright green stripes that you were wearing yesterday in the car park. I might not have seen your face, but I did see those."

Mr Dove glanced down at his feet and back up again.

"And I'll tell her that I was behind your car and I made a scratch on it. That was the noise that alerted you to the fact that someone was listening," Theo lied on the spur of the moment. "There's no way I could've seen or been near your car since but I bet I can describe the shape of the scratch on your car's paint work perfectly. And I know it's your car because I waited by the entrance to the school car park this morning and saw you drive in. It was the same dark green Rover that tried to knock me over."

"I see," Mr Dove said slowly. "I don't think we'll go to see the headmistress after all."

"Er ... I think I'd rather, if it's all the same to you." Theo edged back nervously.

"I've had just about enough of your interfering." Mr Dove took a step forward. "If it wasn't for you and your friends I could've been long gone by now."

"So you admit that you did try to knock me down?"

"I'm only sorry I missed."

Theo took another step backward. Mr Dove took another step forward. It was as if they were both involved in some fearful, macabre dance.

"I know you've got the disks I want. Hand them over and no one will get hurt."

"You mean, *I* won't get hurt."

Mr Dove smiled – an evil, oily smile that

made Theo want to race for the door, but he had to stand his ground.

"Something like that," Mr Dove agreed.

"You've made a mistake, I haven't got the disks."

"I saw them when you emptied your bag on the table earlier." Mr Dove lurched forwards without warning and grabbed Theo by the arm. "Hand over those disks or I will wring your scrawny little neck."

"I don't know what you're talking about..." Theo gasped.

"*Planet of the Anvil* – does that ring any bells?" asked Mr Dove.

"Let go of my arm. You're hurting me."

"Give me your bag. GIVE ME YOUR BAG NOW!" Mr Dove started to shake Theo.

"Here." Theo slipped his duffel bag off his shoulder, but he couldn't stop it from falling on the floor because Mr Dove was still holding his other arm.

Mr Dove released Theo and picked up the bag at once. He started rummaging through it.

"So all this was just to get hold of Jade's

dad's disks?" said Theo.

Mr Dove didn't reply.

"I bet you're not really a teacher at all, are you?"

"As a matter of fact, I am a qualified teacher. It's just not what I do any more. I've found something a lot more lucrative."

"Yeah, like stealing other people's disks."

"It's not the disks. It's what's on them." Mr Dove smirked as he took out a floppy and a CD-ROM from Theo's bag.

"What's so special about an unfinished game?"

"It isn't unfinished. *Planet of the Anvil* is very much complete. And it's going to make us a fortune." Mr Dove waved the disks at Theo. "But there's something else on here that's a lot more important."

"Like what?"

"Like none of your business." Mr Dove tapped his nose. "I'm out of here. And if you know what's good for you, you won't follow me."

Mr Dove headed for the door.

Theo thought for a moment. "Something

that's a lot more important? Oh, I know what you're talking about. You mean the file containing the proof that *Dyna-Cybo Warriors* was Jade's dad's idea and not Alex Reeves'. Yes, I guess that would be more important."

Mr Dove froze in his tracks. He turned, his expression pure rage. "What did you say?"

"Nothing," Theo said quickly. "Didn't you say you had to be going?"

"How d'you know about that file?"

"A friend of mine analysed the disk and managed to break the code and read the files. He's the one who told me that Jade's dad had managed to hack into Alex's computer and retrieve the file with his initial voice notes, as well as the copies of some memos that went back and forth between him and Alex discussing the idea. That's why Jade's dad and Alex had their big quarrel, isn't it? Alex nicked every file referring to the new game from Jade's dad's computer and then passed the game off as his own. It's all in Paul Driscoll's diary file on that floppy disk. The CD contains his new game which he was determined that Alex wouldn't get."

"I think you'd better come with me," Mr Dove said stonily.

"I'd rather not."

Mr Dove made a dive for Theo, but Theo was ready for him and jumped out of the way. He raced towards the door, but Mr Dove was quicker. Just as Theo managed to wrench open the door, Mr Dove's longer arms slammed the door shut. He grabbed Theo's upper arm and squeezed until Theo couldn't feel his fingers.

"You're going to come with me to my car and if you do anything to draw attention to yourself – anything at all – I'll make sure that you are very, very sorry. I hope for your sake that I make myself crystal clear."

Theo gulped and nodded. He tried to prise Mr Dove's fingers off his upper arm but the man wasn't letting go.

"You're hurting me."

"You should've thought about that before you decided to stick your nose in where it wasn't wanted."

"But I'm not the only one who's figured out what's going on." Theo said desperately.

"What's the point of taking me with you?"

"You'll buy us some time." Mr Dove's gaze darted around the classroom like a cornered rat. When he was satisfied that they were really alone, he said, "You're not to say a word to anyone. D'you understand?"

"Yes."

Mr Dove's grip on Theo's arm tightened.

"D'you understand?"

Theo winced and nodded.

"How did you get into our school anyway? I mean, how did you know Mrs Daltry would win a holiday and be away so you could take her place?" Theo gritted his teeth against the pain in his arm. He had to keep talking. He had to wait for a chance to catch Mr Dove off guard.

"Who d'you think arranged for her to win the holiday in the first place?" Mr Dove said scornfully. "Alex and I put up the money. It cost us, but we'll get it back. Jade's dad's new game is going to make us stinking rich."

Theo stared at him. "But … but you couldn't guarantee you'd take her place…"

"Yes, I could. It was just a question of being

in the right place at the right time. I was at the local supply teacher agency when this school rang up for Mrs Daltry's replacement – and here I am. Now no more talking."

Mr Dove opened the door and marched out into the hall, dragging Theo after him. He froze when he saw the crowd in the corridor waiting for him. There stood Jade, Bullet, Ricky, Angela and – looking very perplexed – Mr Appleyard.

"Did you get it?" asked Bullet.

Theo dug into his trouser pocket and before Mr Dove could stop him, he threw a mini tape recorder to Bullet who caught it one handed.

Bullet pressed the OFF button and smiled. Mr Dove looked from Theo to the crowd before him and back again.

"You..."

"Every word," Theo grinned. "Now let go of my arm."

In a daze Mr Dove did as Theo ordered.

"What's going on?" Mr Appleyard was annoyed. "I thought you said there was a rat up in the classroom."

"There is. You're looking at him," Bullet replied. "Could you make sure he doesn't go anywhere while I get one of the teachers to call the police?"

Without waiting for a reply, Bullet raced down the corridor to the staff room.

"You're the new supply teacher. Mr Dove, isn't it?" asked the caretaker.

"He's not a teacher at all. He tried to knock me over," said Theo.

"You're not going to believe the word of these kids over me, are you?" Mr Dove laughed lightly.

Mr Appleyard's eyes narrowed. "I know these kids. And while they get on my nerves, I don't think they'd lie about something like this. Not something that could get them into so much trouble if it was a lie. But on the other hand, I don't know you from a hole in the ground! So I think you'd better stay exactly where you are."

If Mr Appleyard had looked around at that moment and seen the looks on the faces of Theo and the others, his head would've doubled in size. Theo was amazed. Mr

Appleyard was actually going to help them. Theo had always planned with Bullet that he'd do something to get kept behind by Mr Dove. The plan was for Bullet to get Mr Appleyard the moment the class was over. Theo reckoned the caretaker was a better bet than one of the teachers who would never believe anything against another teacher. But Mr Appleyard's reaction was always the biggest worry. He could've turned round and called them all liars. As it was, Mr Appleyard's suspicious, wary eyes were still on Mr Dove.

Mr Dove looked up and down the corridor. Quick as a snap, he made a break for it, racing for the stairs at the end of the corridor.

"Oh no you don't!" Mr Appleyard was the first to move. He chased after Mr Dove, but it was Angela who rugby tackled Mr Dove to the floor. Theo, Ricky and Mr Appleyard piled on top of him to make sure he couldn't get up and try to escape again.

"Get off me! GET… OFF… ME!" Mr Dove yelled.

"Yeah, right!" Ricky scoffed.

Jade walked up and around them to look

down at the squirming ex-teacher.

"You're the one who sent me all those mail messages, aren't you?"

Mr Dove didn't reply.

"You must've found out Dad's password and you've been sending me emails pretending to be him. How could you? How could you be so mean?"

"You had something we wanted," Mr Dove sneered, not in the least bit repentant.

Jade gave him a look that could sour milk. She drew herself up to her full height and looked at Mr Dove as if he was something nasty she had just stepped in. "I've just figured it out. You work for Alex, don't you?" Jade asked.

"Who's Alex?" Mr Dove said curtly.

"Don't worry," Theo told Jade. "The tape proves he does know Alex Reeves."

"Even if I do, you can't prove she had anything to do with this," said Mr Dove.

"She?" Theo was astounded. And he wasn't the only one.

"Jade, you never said that Alex Reeves was a woman," said Angela.

"Didn't I? I thought I did," Jade replied.

"Is she a tall, pretty woman with dark brown hair down to her shoulders?" Theo asked.

Jade nodded. "Why? D'you know her?"

"She was with him when they tried to knock me over," said Theo.

"My sister's much too smart for any of you," Mr Dove scoffed. "By the time she's told her side of the story, the police will think you're crazy."

"Your sister?" Jade whispered.

"I should've guessed. Well, I might not have seen your face yesterday evening, but I did see hers – more than once," Theo reminded Mr Dove. "And with that tape and everything you just said, I think I'll manage to convince the police."

"And Theo, don't forget, Angela and I saw her too," said Ricky. "We saw her take the package out of the bin in the precinct."

Mr Dove's face fell. Bullet came running down the corridor with at least three other teachers behind him.

"Mr Appleyard, just what d'you think you're doing? Get off Mr Dove at once – and that goes for the rest of you," Mr Cookson ordered.

"Not a chance," Mr Appleyard replied. "Not until the police get here."

Mr Cookson looked around and frowned deeply. "Would someone mind telling me exactly what's going on?"

# 18. Friends

Ricky, Theo, Angela, Jade and Bullet all sat around the same lunch table. They were very aware of the looks they were getting from the rest of the dining-hall.

"This has got my detective agency off to a flying start," Theo said with relish.

"Whose detective agency?" Angela raised an eyebrow.

"*Our* detective agency," Theo amended.

"Are you still going through with that? Haven't you had enough excitement to last you a lifetime?" Jade frowned.

"Nah! I'm just getting into it," Theo grinned. "Besides, with the five of us in this detective agency, there won't be a case we won't be able to crack."

"The five of us? You mean ... you mean, I'm included?" Bullet asked amazed.

"Of course you are. You're our computer expert," Theo said with impatience. "I thought that was obvious."

"I'm included." Bullet grinned around the table.

"I'm the brains of the outfit," Theo continued. "Bullet can be the computer expert, Angela can be the heavy and do all the strong arm stuff..."

"Thanks!" Angela said, indignantly.

"Ricky will be the second lot of brains and Jade can look after the girlie problems." Theo's grin was even broader. "I've got it all worked out."

"Girlie problems? That is outrageous! What a cheek!" Angela's indignation knew no bounds now.

"OK, brains! If you're so clever, tell me how Mr Dove knew that I'd told you about the emails I was getting," Jade challenged.

"That's easy," Theo grinned. "Remember when you first came up to us in the corridor and asked if we believed in ghosts? And d'you remember how Mr Dove passed us in the corridor and we all shut up until he turned the corner? Well, I reckon he turned the corner but he didn't carry on walking to the staff room. I think he just stood there and listened to our conversation. He probably guessed what you had on your mind. And then when you took us to your house, I was sure we were being followed..."

"You never said!" Ricky frowned.

"I thought maybe I was imagining things, but now I don't think so. I think Mr Dove was behind us. That's how he knew you'd confided in us, Jade," said Theo. "I mean, what else would we be doing at your house?"

Jade looked at Theo, impressed. "Theo, you just might make a detective yet!"

Theo nodded happily. Nothing could dampen his mood. Mr Dove had been taken away by the police and although they'd had to spend the rest of the morning explaining what had happened, it seemed like Mr Dove and his sister were definitely going to get what they deserved. The police wanted each of them to go round to the local police station within the next twenty-four hours with their parents to make official statements. Theo was more than willing. He was just a bit worried about how he was going to explain the whole thing to his mum and dad first.

"You'll all be glad to know that I think I've finally got my Crimebuster program working, so it's at your disposal, Theo," Bullet announced. "It's just a shame it had a couple of bugs in it before this, or it might have led you to the truth sooner."

"And then again..." Theo teased.

"Just a minute, Theo," said Ricky. "I've got a huge Tyrannosaurus Rex bone to pick with you."

Theo sighed. Was he the only one who was *happy* about the outcome?

"Go on, then," Theo said, his head resting on one of his hands.

"Just what did you think you were doing by not telling me what was going on?"

"You and Angela have already been through enough, don't you think? It wouldn't have been fair to drag you into this – especially if I was wrong about Mr Dove. I didn't want to get the two of you into any more trouble after everything you went through during the kidnapping incident."

"Theo, that wasn't your decision to make," Angela said angrily. "You should've told me and Ricky what was going on and let us make up our own minds."

"Too right!" Ricky agreed.

"But you wouldn't have said no, even if you wanted to," Theo shrugged.

"Theo, don't you ever do that again," Ricky said, his voice so quiet that Theo almost didn't hear what he said.

Everyone else around the table grew quiet too. They could all tell that Ricky was furiously angry.

"We're friends. You don't shut friends out like that," Ricky fumed.

"But I was only doing it *because* we're friends." Theo tried to defend himself.

"I told him that he should tell both of you what was going on," said Jade. "But he wouldn't listen."

"He does tend to think he knows everything, doesn't he?" Bullet added.

"What is this? Get at Theo hour?" Theo said indignantly. "Anyone else?"

"I mean it, Theo." Ricky still wasn't mollified. "Don't you ever do that again? Do you understand?"

Theo nodded. "Are we friends again?"

It took a few moments, but at last Ricky nodded.

"Then why do you still have a face like a handful of mince?" Theo teased.

Reluctantly, Ricky smiled. Theo realized that it was going to take a while for Ricky to fully forgive him – but he would. Bullet turned to Jade.

"I'm sorry about what I said about the email messages you were getting," Bullet said seriously. "I never meant to upset you."

"I know that." Jade managed a smile. "It wasn't your fault. It was just a bit... I'll be all right. It'll take a while, but I'll be all right."

Silence.

Theo tried to think of something to change the subject. "Oh, are you going to get in touch with Pascoe DeMille then? He was hanging around the school earlier, probably looking for you."

"That's not funny, Theo. In fact I think it was very cruel of all of you to play a trick on me like that," said Jade.

Bewildered, Theo looked at his friends but from the expressions on their faces they were at as much of a loss as he was.

"You know what I'm talking about," said Jade.

"I haven't a clue," Theo denied.

"Pascoe DeMille," Jade said impatiently. "You know very well that years and years ago my dad tried acting for a while before he went into computing. That was before I was even born and a long time before we moved to our current house. His stage name was Pascoe DeMille. He used the same initials as in his real name."

Paul Driscoll... Pascoe DeMille...

Theo stared at Jade in stunned silence. He wasn't the only one.

"Are you saying..." Angela's voice came out in a high-pitched squeak. She coughed and tried again. "Are you saying that Pascoe

DeMille is … was your *dad*?"

"Of course not," Jade replied. She looked around the table. "If you lot aren't having me on, then someone's playing a joke on *you*."

"D'you have a photograph of your dad?" Ricky asked quietly.

Jade nodded. "I've got lots of photos."

"Can we see them?"

Jade dug into her bag and took out a tatty envelope. She emptied its contents over the table. Family photographs fanned out everywhere. There were photos of Jade's dad by himself, photos of Jade and her mum and dad on holiday, in the house, in the garden. Theo could understand Jade carrying around all those photos. In her shoes he would do the same. After a moment's hesitation, everyone reached out to pick up the photos for a closer look.

"I didn't get to see this Pascoe DeMille person." Bullet looked at the photos with interest. "Did he make himself up to look like Jade's dad then?"

Ricky, Angela and Theo looked at each other. Theo felt a chill trickle down his back then snake its icy way through the rest of his body.

"Jade, the man who spoke to us, the man who helped us – it was this guy." Ricky pointed to the man in the photograph he was holding. "There's no doubt about it. The man we met was a lot younger, but it was definitely this man."

"It can't have been. That's my dad." Jade frowned deeply.

"I know," said Theo. "It all makes sense. That's why he was helping us. We must've been talking to your dad's gh…"

"Theo," Angela interrupted. "Do me a favour and don't finish that sentence."

"Wow!" Ricky breathed. "It's just like when I was in Scotland with Mum and one morning, I was downstairs in the dining-room and I saw…"

"Ricky," Theo raised a hand. "No more ghost stories. I think I've heard enough about ghosts to last me a lifetime."

And for once, no one argued.

# HIPPO GHOST

## Summer Visitors

Emma thinks she's in for a really boring summer, until she meets the Carstairs family on the beach. But there's something very *strange* about her new friends. . .

*Carol Barton*

## Ghostly Music

Beth loves her piano lessons. So why have they started to make her *ill*. . . ?

*Richard Brown*

## A Patchwork of Ghosts

Who is the evil-looking ghost tormenting Lizzie, and why does he want to hurt her...?

*Angela Bull*

## The Ghosts who Waited

Everything's changed since Rosy and her family moved house. Why has everyone suddenly turned against her. . .?

*Dennis Hamley*

## The Railway Phantoms

Rachel has visions. She dreams of two children in strange, disintegrating clothes. And it seems as if they are trying to contact her...

*Dennis Hamley*

## The Haunting of Gull Cottage

Unless Kezzie and James can find what really happened in Gull Cottage that terrible night many years ago, the haunting may never stop...

*Tessa Krailing*

## The Hidden Tomb

Can Kate unlock the mystery of the curse on Middleton Hall, before it destroys the Mason family...?

*Jenny Oldfield*

## The House at the End of Ferry Road

The house at the end of Ferry Road has just been built. So it can't be haunted, can it...?

*Martin Oliver*

## Beware! This House is Haunted
## This House is Haunted Too!

Jessica doesn't believe in ghosts. So who *is* writing the strange, spooky messages?

*Lance Salway*

## The Children Next Door

Laura longs to make friends with the children next door. But they're not quite what they seem. . .

*Jean Ure*

# HIPPO ANIMAL

*Have you ever longed for a puppy to love, or a horse of your own? Have you ever wondered what it would be like to make friends with a wild animal? If so, then you're sure to fall in love with these fantastic titles from Hippo Animal!*

## Thunderfoot

*Deborah van der Beek*

When Mel finds the enormous, neglected horse Thunderfoot, she doesn't know it will change her life for ever...

## Vanilla Fudge

*Deborah van der Beek*

When Lizzie and Hannah fall in love with the same dog, neither of them will give up without a fight...

## A Foxcub Named Freedom

*Brenda Jobling*

An injured vixen nudges her young son away from her. She can sense danger and cares nothing for herself – only for her son's freedom...

## Goose on the Run

*Brenda Jobling*

It's an unusual pet – an injured Canada goose. But soon Josh can't imagine being without him. And the goose won't let *anyone* take him away from Josh. . .

## Pirate the Seal

*Brenda Jobling*

Ryan's always been lonely – but then he meets Pirate and at last he has a real friend...

## Animal Rescue

*Bette Paul*

Can Tessa help save the badgers of Delves Wood from destruction?

## Take Six Puppies

*Bette Paul*

Anna knows she shouldn't get attached to the six new puppies at the Millington Farm Dog Sanctuary, but surely it can't hurt to get just a *little* bit fond of them...

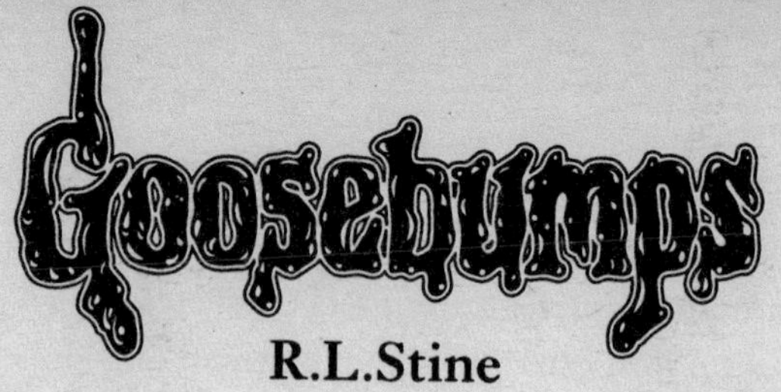

R.L.Stine

Reader beware, you're in for a scare!

These terrifying tales will send shivers up your spine:

1 Welcome to Dead House
2 Say Cheese and Die!
3 Stay Out of the Basement
4 The Curse of the Mummy's Tomb
5 Monster Blood
6 Let's Get Invisible
7 Night of the Living Dummy
8 The Girl Who Cried Monster
9 Welcome to Camp Nightmare
10 The Ghost Next Door
11 The Haunted Mask
12 Piano Lessons Can Be Murder
13 Be Careful What You Wish For
14 The Werewolf of Fever Swamp
15 You Can't Scare Me
16 One Day at HorrorLand
17 Why I'm Afraid of Bees
18 Monster Blood II
19 Deep Trouble
20 Go Eat Worms
21 Return of the Mummy
22 The Scarecrow Walks at Midnight
23 Attack of the Mutant
24 My Hairiest Adventure
25 A Night in Terror Tower

The Cuckoo Clock of Doom
Monster Blood III
Ghost Beach
Phantom of the Auditorium
30 It Came From Beneath the Sink!
31 Night of the Living Dummy II
32 The Barking Ghost
33 The Horror at Camp Jellyjam
34 Revenge of the Garden Gnomes
35 A Shocker on Shock Street
36 The Haunted Mask II
37 The Headless Ghost
38 The Abominable Snowman of Pasadena
39 How I Got My Shrunken Head
40 Night of the Living Dummy III
41 Bad Hare Day
42 Egg Monsters From Mars
43 The Beast From the East
44 Say Cheese and Die – Again!
45 Ghost Camp